Advance Praise

"A fast-paced thriller involving intelligence agency conspiracies, forged dossiers, and media complicity. It makes for exciting fiction, but thank goodness nothing like this could ever actually happen...."

—Glenn Reynolds, the Beauchamp Brogan Distinguished Professor of Law at the University of Tennessee College of Law, who is known for his political blog Instapundit

"Frank Miniter has given us a real hero for this political age. Sidney McDaniel is so compelling—and important right now—that he's a character I'd like to play."

—Kevin Sorbo, Actor, Director, Producer, and Author

"Frank Miniter's ability to weave words that thrill, to take us on a breathtaking journey are at full tilt in this book. A riveting read for both the politically savvy and the those who just want to be taken on a ride."

—Hollie McKay, Author of *Only Cry for the Living*, Journalist, and Geopolitical Specialist

"Sid McDaniel is a hero for our time, willing to go head-to-head in cyber combat against our would-be puppet masters in Frank Miniter's superb *The Deep State Revolution*."

—Stephen Hunter, Author of the Bestselling Bob Lee Swagger Series of Thrillers

Also by Frank Miniter

Spies in Congress:
Inside the Democrats' Covered-Up Cyber Scandal

Conquer Anything:
A Green Beret's Guide to Building Your A-Team

Kill Big Brother

THE DEEP STATE REVOLUTION

FRANK MINITER

PERMUTED PRESS

A PERMUTED PRESS BOOK
ISBN: 978-1-63758-078-3
ISBN (eBook): 978-1-63758-079-0

Cover design by Brad Walker

PERMUTED
PRESS

Permuted Press, LLC
New York • Nashville
permutedpress.com

Published in the United States of America
1 2 3 4 5 6 7 8 9 10

To every real whistleblower devoured by the Deep State.

CHAPTER 1

"What journalist lives like this?"

The question from Mack Davis, opinion editor of the *New York Herald*, saunters across the spacious first-floor living room of a nineteenth-century, Uptown Manhattan brownstone and nudges a smile out of Sid McDaniel.

Sid sinks back into the ornate white sofa, his legs crossed and his arms stretched across the top, waiting patiently for Mack to get to what might as well be a ticking time bomb between them.

Across the room, Mack is on the edge of an identical white sofa, only he's all lit up like Times Square as he speaks with his hands moving and his eyes darting.

"Are you some kind of combination of Bruce Wayne and Clark Kent? Are you just waiting here for an emergency beacon so you can spin into a superhero to save the city?"

Sid shrugs and offers another easy smile. He knows this room, even the entire building, is an opulent front. He chose and carefully decorated the place to give both his friends and his enemies pause.

Still, he likes that, despite its old-money feel, this building is comfortably filled with wide-open rooms you can have a whole thought in. Indeed, it fits him wonderfully as both a home and an office in this grand, dirty, corrupt, dangerous, complicated, rotting city. It is just close enough to Wall Street for him to take the subway downtown to do his undercover work for Fortune 500s that have been hacked, shackled with ransomware, or infiltrated by foreign spies doing corporate espionage—and it is just far enough from all of that to give him perspective.

"What I mean," Mack continues, as if he is addressing an audience, "is this place is almost a museum set of an early twentieth-century man's Uptown pad. But then there's that modern-looking spiral staircase right in the middle. I think you should take out that staircase and put in a fire pole, Batman, so you can slide down when some siren goes off."

Sid shrugs again, without taking his arms off the top of the couch. Clearly, given just a little time, a scotch or two, and some flattery, he could get Mack to talk and talk and so would learn nearly anything the editor has to tell. But there isn't time for that, so he says, "Just keep me off page six."

"Gonna be hard," says Mack, smiling broadly for emphasis. Then he sighs and says, "Sid, you're like an old-fashioned, reluctant movie sleuth. Like Nick Charles, but without Nora and the Jack Russell—just tripping along good-naturedly into wealth and scandal."

"Sans the martinis this morning," Sid replies with a chuckle.

Mack rubs his chin, nods agreement, and says, "In this place, I do feel like I should have a touch of brandy in my coffee."

"That can be arranged."

Sid is enjoying his editor's practiced flamboyance, as honest as a child playing a card game. He even likes that Mack takes his look right out of *GQ*. He has his suit jacket off without a tie, his collar unbuttoned two down, and his pink shirtsleeves rolled up, showing off a silver watch almost as shiny as his whitened teeth. His receding hair is dark and slicked back with too much product, causing the top of his head to reflect the chandelier's white light. He thinks this look on Mack showcases a kind of predictable conformity that can be trusted. This man, after all, isn't a walking fraud. He clearly isn't unsure of who he is. He is a veteran editor, adept at finding, and then drawing out, sordid tales across weeks, or even months, of scintillating coverage that almost brings a story to a climax, over and over—before pulling back again and promising more in the next edition.

For his part, Mack is excited about this developing story. It's like a scandalous novel—all about what a sitting president, and his family, did and didn't do in a previous administration and in his campaign. It has intrigue, espionage, possible coming court actions, and foreign governments that can and will protect their interests. It has an FBI investigation, an active coverup, and both political parties caught up in its salivating clown grin. And, unlike the previous dossier on a sitting president, this one is being suppressed by the U.S. intelligence agencies, which gives the aching scandal a drip-drip, conspiratorial flavor.

Meanwhile, this tech guru sitting in front of him—who is also the *Herald's* most-popular columnist—is somehow central to this delicious affair.

With all of this as background, Mack isn't sure how to even begin this explosive conversation, which is why he is dodging around behind classic film references. He certainly didn't expect this silent treatment. Not knowing Sid firsthand, he expected forgettable, if nervous, small talk—first over coffee, then a feeling-out process that would border on an interrogation before they really got into it. As it is now, he really isn't sure how to proceed. He knows that amateurs immediately seek conclusions or answers, whereas a good editor at an urban newspaper is a tease, a dramatist, and a lovable sort of con artist, all in one. Mack has worked to become all of those things, and now those skills are simply a part of him.

So he makes a big show of taking in the room's hand-painted Iksel wallpaper; its marble fireplace, unlighted on this lovely spring morning; its three-leaded, stained-glass French doors: one leading to a walled garden filled with budding red roses; another to a bijou powder room; and the last to a service kitchen, where someone is clanking white porcelain cups onto silver as they gather coffee, butter, and brioche. His eyes finally settle on a chessboard sitting on a marble-topped coffee table between them. The board is filled with dark and light stained squares. Its black-and-white marble rooks, bishops, kings, and queens match the table, and the pieces are in play. A few have already been taken. He wonders if it's just there for show as he raises his eyes to Sid.

"Playing against yourself?"

"Someone online, a fast-chess champion. Ironically, we had to stop suddenly, but we'll pick it up again."

Mack decides not to pursue the topic as he continues to take the measure of this tech-whiz kid who calls this museum home, or headquarters, or something. Given what is going on, he thinks Sid looks too relaxed in loafers, linen pants, and a white polo. The man's posture is both casually disarming and self-confident. It's as if Sid's body is saying he doesn't have a care in the world, while his eyes are saying he's really a lion in the long grass. He can't quite figure out what gives Sid this aura. Arrogance? That doesn't fit. Sid doesn't talk about himself. He doesn't even want to be talked about. Naivete doesn't fit either. This man seems anything but naive.

But dammit, he should be more upset, more vulnerable. He may well be a lion in the grass, but truckloads of hunters are coming for him. Doesn't he know he could lose everything? A lot of powerful people want him to take the bullet for this dossier.

As they eye each other, a woman's heels come clicking down the spiral staircase and onto the wide planks of the hardwood floor between them. Her dark hair is up, and she is in midnight-blue slacks and a red satin blouse tailored to her athletic figure. She wears black-framed eyeglasses. Her complexion is Latin, and a scent wafts in with her. *Bulgari?*

She smiles at him before handing Sid a tablet device.

"Need your signature."

Sid looks it over, nods, and signs.

Mack's eyes follow her figure as her heels click back up the wooden spiral staircase to the second floor. When he turns back to Sid, he sees that Sid has been watching him watching *her*, amused.

"Was that Lois Lane?"

Sid smiles. "Gloria is an accomplished attorney."

Mack raises his chin, incredulous.

"She was a fighter pilot in the Navy," Sid says simply. "She got out with an earned disdain for male chauvinism and went to Yale Law. She graduated from that elite academic institution with a healthy distrust of the bureaucratic system and decided to practice civil-liberties litigation. She wound up in a nonprofit with people more detached from the real world than even those in academia. She came to me after that whole Verity incident and told me she wanted to do something real; she wanted to apply old-fashioned freedom to the new tech world. She is doing that now. I'm lucky to have her here."

"Lucky all around," Mack replies.

A thirty-something Hispanic man with the physique of a personal trainer comes into the room through a swinging kitchen door. He places a silver tray on the coffee table, beside the chess board, and asks Mack, "Coffee?"

"Please."

"Nothing for me, Jorge," says Sid.

Jorge pours steaming coffee into a small white cup on a saucer and leaves it on the tray next to cream, strawberry jam, and warm croissants.

"Where'd you find him?" Mack asks after the man disappears.

"Jorge? Oh, he spent ten years on a Green Beret A-Team. His specialty was intelligence—eavesdropping on enemy communications, hacking systems, running surveillance equipment, and gathering intel. He has been training me in mixed martial arts and some small arms tactical stuff. We've even done some 3-gun competitions together—you know, timed stuff with AR-type rifles, pistols, and shotguns on scenario-based courses. He can still move, too, though he had a piece of Humvee steel the size of a saucer go through his gut from a roadside bomb in Afghanistan. He should have died. No one thought he had a chance. He told me he even saw a medic shaking his head and waving his hand under his chin after another Green Beret—and this during a firefight—asked if he'd make it until a chopper got there. After a year in a hospital in San Antonio, they retired him. Rather than take a desk job somewhere, he came to me, thanks to a shared contact. He's invaluable. I like him close."

"Quite the team. How about that lithe fellow in the dark suit who took my phone at the door?"

"Adam. He's Israeli. He was in Mossad. Worked in embassies mostly. That's all I can say about him."

"How'd he come to you?"

"Oh, I met him on a job, a Wall Street-listed firm that had been hacked. The malware was directing a tiny fraction of profits to an offshore account. The guilty party was an Israeli national."

"Was?"

Sid shrugs.

Mack Davis swallows his next question, knowing Sid has told him all he will, but also wondering why he had told him anything at all.

This pause gives them a moment more to consider each other. Mack thinks Sid is too young for his resumé. *Is he even thirty years old?* As they eye each other, still circling and feinting, Mack opts to jab to the body.

"Look, Sid. We run your column. We're the only paper in New York that would, but it would help if you'd stick to a schedule—say, a column every Wednesday."

"Schedules force things. I can't force out the facts."

"Well, then, how about at least giving us a heads-up once in a while?"

"I don't want the pressure of expectation."

Mack drops the smile. "You sure are a strange sort of columnist." He glances aside for an instant, as if checking the countdown clock on the time bomb they're both ignoring. He looks back at Sid, unsure how to broach the topic without shouting, "It's gonna blow!" So he stalls with: "Our readers would like to know more about you."

Sid nods and looks down, in a manner some would take for bashful humility, but that Mack decides is an act. He knows he has been allowed in this room only because someone leaked that Sid McDaniel is involved in what Washington's chattering classes are calling "The Dirty Document": an unflattering fifty-one pages of opposition research into the president. Word is Sid's digital fingerprints are all over the sordid thing. But as yet, neither Mack nor any other journalist has been able to verify this, or to get sources to back up the many dirty details within it—such as its claims of seedy and unscrupulously lucrative activities the president and his family allegedly had with foreign governments and state-controlled corporations.

Sid had been tipped about his own alleged involvement in the so-called Dirty Document just a few days before. Now he needs more, and he needs it fast, as any connection to this—even a false one—could destroy his firm. Still, impatient as he feels, he has learned not to push people with words. It's always better to prompt them with silence and presence. If you give them quiet moments, most people get nervous and start saying what's really on their minds. Whereas if you push them, if you bully them with tough talk, they often get apprehensive or mad and shut up. As Sid eyes Mack, he is sure this editor won't tell him a thing in the few remaining minutes they have together, but he is just as sure Mack will give him everything he needs.

And he needs a lot, fast. Sid devoted the whole past weekend to digging into the dossier's metadata and tracing it to its sources. His team spent the past two nights here, napping occasionally on these couches, trying to understand who is behind this and what these people want. He has yet to answer even those basic questions. But they found that its sources do point to him, though it is too obvious a setup. No one in cyber security would believe Sid McDaniel wouldn't cloak his own IP address. Only the media would swallow and push such a blatant frame. But why would they even want to pursue this story? The president is a Democrat.

So, is this an NSA attempt to discredit and destroy him? The National Security Agency does have the ability to change metadata—that revelation came out years ago from the mysterious group Shadow Brokers. They leaked a lot of the NSA's top-secret tools, including EternalBlue, a worm weaponized to use a transport protocol that allows Windows machines to communicate. It can alter even the data that show when and from where a signal came in. That means a lot of the big players are likely now to be able to change these digital fingerprints. And, after that Verity affair, the NSA does have reason to take him down. The RNC and DNC don't have this kind of sophistication, but some of the firms they hire might. Then again, maybe it was a foreign government. The Russians. The Chinese. This Dirty Document is all about Russian and Chinese connections, and the Russians do love sowing discord with counterintelligence plants. He has enemies in both governments, as he has spent a decade now working undercover for corporations to defeat cyber threats and corporate espionage, which are mostly from Russia and China.

Sid knows editors like Mack Davis are at the center of gossip storms. They hear things, are leaked saucy details, and broadcast these rumors in social-media campaigns, in the hope they will make articles go viral—all to push ad dollars. Many things they put out there are factual, at least in part, while others are hearsay; the only thing they are really scared of is being obviously libelous, but still, all of the information matters.

Mack is tired of waiting for an answer. "Well? Are you going to let us tell our subscribers something about you, or not?"

"Photos of me are off limits," says Sid carefully.

"Yes, I'm familiar with your contract. Your security person, Adam, even took my phone at the door."

"A necessary precaution."

"You don't want to be a known face, I get that. But there are photos of you out there."

"Some. Most are misinformation."

"You put them out there?" Mack is smiling again.

"A celebrity," says Sid as he shakes his head, "for me, that's too invasive a part to play."

Mack leans toward him and asks, "Well, okay. I'll get to the point. You invited me here. Why?"

"You know why."

The editor is no longer smiling. He stands and starts to pace along the broad planks of the hardwood floor between the sofas.

"It's bad. Bad." He stops, looks at Sid. "Any truth to it?"

"Do I seem like a political operative to you?"

"You, no. But you *are* a mystery." Mack is pacing again. "Your column is always so spot on. We've stopped doubting your facts. They're uncannily accurate. You must have a lot of sources in both parties. Yet you never care about the politics. You don't take sides. You take the spin out of the story of the day, and you write in this authoritative style that reads like true confessions from the political class. People fear you. But our audience adores you. I don't have to tell you that you are by far our most popular columnist."

"I'm glad. And now I need something from you."

Mack pauses, hands on hips, looking into the small rose garden. Then he turns back to face Sid, shaking his head. "We don't, we can't, give up sources."

"Of course," says Sid. "Regardless, I already have a lot on this now. I should have a column to you in a few days, one that'll blow this thing up."

Sid stands, extends his right hand, and says, "Thanks for coming, Mack. I've long wanted to meet you in person. I'm sorry this visit has been so short, but, as you know, I have a problem to get to the bottom of."

Mack shakes Sid's hand and, though he didn't hear him come in, Jorge is suddenly on his left, guiding him out. He is led out of a door that closes with an air lock swoosh and into a small room where Adam is waiting with his phone.

Soon he is outside the second door and walking again down West Seventy-Sixth Street. It's a warm and pleasant spring morning. He looks back up at the brownstone and realizes, for the first time, that all of the windows are reflecting the newly leafed-out trees lining the street, and the red of the other brick buildings. He can't see into any of them. *That place is built like the U.S. embassy in Iran.*

He looks at his phone, sees missed calls and texts. His first call is to his boss.

"He wanted to know who tipped us."

"Oh," says the executive editorial page director. "He knows we can't do that."

"But should we be going with this story? We might lose our top columnist."

"We'll wait, but Senator Haskins needs to hear something or he'll place it elsewhere. We'll tell him we're waiting for a second source."

"Sid also said he'll have something big for us on this soon. He called it explosive."

"Can't wait to see that," says his boss. "But the public doesn't know about any of this yet. They'll need a narrative. We have to get that ready. Come to my office when you get here. We have to talk about how to make this intelligible to the masses. Maybe with a multi-part series."

After listening to this conversation in real time, thanks to a little piece of software added to the editor's cell, Sid deletes the hack from the phone, then sits in a leather swivel chair in his third-floor office. He looks out a bright window at a green, budding maple tree, with red brick buildings beyond. Then he leans back into the chair and puts his feet up on the type of old wooden desk Phillip Marlowe would have sat behind.

"Okay," he says, turning to Gloria. "Tell the RNC front man I'll meet him this afternoon. It was a Republican senator."

CHAPTER 2

Early Monday afternoon a fat man in an off-the-rack gray flannel suit has his elbows planted on stiff white linen. The linen is smothering a little square table in a room of little square tables. This man's bald head has sweat drops beading above floppy ears. His eyes bulge like a goldfish's as he stares out of the restaurant's front window, inspecting every face in the passing parade on the Fifth Avenue sidewalk.

The man had specifically asked for table five, just as he was told to in a text message received minutes before. The two waiters in the back don't know why he wanted table five and don't care. The place is nearly empty and they'd never seen him before. All he ordered was coffee, which did annoy them, but then it is late for lunch and too early for dinner. He can sit till dinner, for all they care. The only other people in the room are two tourists giggling as they struggle with the Italian menus.

As his eyes scan the passers-by, all the fat man can think is: This must work. It *must*.

His party's involvement in this "Dirty Document" debacle could blow up everything. And it's too late for that, much too late.

The time to stop this guy from becoming president has passed. Now they must hold their tongues, play defense, and wait for the next election. Power will come back to them. It always has.

They just can't let the public know they had their fingers in this mess. This is too politically volatile. This thing could burn everything down. All that would be left would be the machine-gun staccato of cable news pundits cackling as they point out how extreme the Republican Party has become.

Someone will publish it sooner or later, of course. It is too delicious, too scandalous, too filled with graphic details for the news sites—so desperate for clickbait—to resist, despite what their lawsuit-adverse lawyers will tell them. But that'll be manageable, if they have enough to create a counter-narrative about their involvement.

Their immediate problem, however, is the person with his digital fingerprints all over this dossier. He's an infamous tech guru do-gooder. The man is half myth. He has no ties or loyalties, no family. Worst of all, he is a man with no politics, at least none they can discern. He is a registered independent who votes all over the spectrum. He certainly doesn't need money, but he has never given a dime to either party or even to some revealing cause or another. There are charities on his federal tax forms, of course, but nothing ideological.

Who can trust somebody like that? How do you control a character like that? How do you even *talk* to a man like that?

Getting a clean photo of this guy, this Sid McDaniel, hasn't been easy. He looks so different in every available photo that no one could pick him out of a lineup, though the FBI assures them they are all of McDaniel.

Suddenly, and right on time, he sees a man's face above the crowd. The man has stopped and is staring at him through the front window of the restaurant. He is tall and lean, maybe forty. He wears a well-tailored suit, wrap-around sunglasses, and a stern expression, with a few days of stubble on his cheeks and a head buzzed to a dark shadow.

His eyes follow the man as he moves to the restaurant door and enters.

Adam glances at the only other two patrons in the restaurant. He then looks over the two waiters. One is leaning on the bar running along a side wall, the other against the back wall.

Satisfied, he takes off his sunglasses and turns to the fat GOP operative at table five, looking him up and down. The man smiles up at him stupidly and starts to rise, but then stops, looking nervous.

"That's right, get up," says Adam.

The fat man's chair squeaks on black-and-white-checkered tile as he stands.

Adam approaches the man and with a few quick, invasive motions uses his scanner to check him for weapons and transmitter signals. A beep leads to the pocket where he finds a phone. He reaches into the pocket, pulls out the phone, and finds it recording. Adam orders the man to stop the recording. After he does, Adam takes the phone, steps back, and softly says, "All clear," before walking back outside, bringing the phone with him.

A moment later the door opens again, and lovely April air and taxi horns blow in with another man. The door shuts behind him with a thud, and the Manhattan street sounds return to muted background noise.

This man's sunglasses are aviators. Unlike the other guy, his face is unfashionably clean-shaven. His shoes are brown Italian monk straps, and his pants are a light tan linen. His shirt is a simple white, short-sleeve polo, untucked.

He carries no bag. He is dressed too casually to be an office worker. He is too empty- handed to be a tourist.

Looking up at him from the table, Bob Steward knows exactly who he is.

Sid makes his way between the tables and extends his hand as Steward rises. Without a word, they shake hands. He finds Steward's hand to be too soft, too moist.

Sid pulls out a dark wooden chair and sits comfortably, turning slightly toward the window to let the spring sunshine fall over him. He takes off his sunglasses, places them on the table, and crosses his legs.

He doesn't want to be here. He never meets sources like this. He uses encrypted conversations, with video when possible, through an app he built, so he can read emotions, so his software can look for deception—and so the other person can't set up a hit on him. He especially doesn't like being here with this operative from what was once the Grand Old Party. It always felt like guilt by association to meet with a drone from either party, and he knows this meeting could be brought up later to insinuate anything. But since he has to be here, Sid decides to look beneath this man's Potemkin front.

Steward's forehead is shiny and his fat mouth partly open under a droopy mustache. His knees splay out from the necessity his stomach imposes—a real man-spreader—and his stubby fingers nervously grip a cup of coffee. His eyes are cynical but expectant, and are above bags of loose skin. He looks like someone who rushed from Penn Station after a morning on the Acela, which Sid suspects is probably the case.

Sid has done his homework about this guy. Bob Steward has been slowly rising within the Republican National Committee since he was in his early twenties. He is known as "Just Bob"—a trustworthy nobody who gets sensitive things done. That's because he doesn't have the capacity for creativity, which is what makes him trustworthy and therefore useful to the savvier minds in RNC leadership.

A waiter moves up to Sid's right shoulder.

"Good afternoon," Sid greets him. "An espresso, please."

The waiter fades away.

Sid looks back at the man across the table and raises his eyebrows to invite him to speak.

"Thank you for coming," says Steward with an anxious half-smile. "We know you don't like in-person meetings."

Steward pauses, waiting for Sid to say something polite to ease the tension. Sid just waits him out. When the silence gets too uncomfortable, Steward says, "I have some sources who might be useful to you."

Sid remains silent as the waiter's hand reaches between them and sets an espresso on the white linen before moving away.

"The waiters here are very European," Sid says finally, sipping the espresso in such a calm, deliberate manner that he knew Steward would be pushed even more off balance. "The French waiters, I can take them. Of course, they wait on you only as much as they feel obligated to, but at least they don't look at you like cynical teens, as so many Americans do. And they really do know about the food and the wine, whereas their American counterparts more often just memorize a list. Still, in my experience, the Italians are better. They know how to be there without being there."

Silence again, this time for fifteen seconds. Steward blinks uncertainly, then begins again. "My sources tell me—"

Sid raises his right hand. "I know what you want to tell me. I am meeting you for another reason entirely."

After a pause of thirty seconds, Steward ventures, "You are known as a journalist who prints the facts, and yet—"

"What do you mean by 'journalist'?" Sid asks calmly, taking another sip.

"Someone who prints what they think to be true."

"Come now, do you really think that is what journalists do today?"

Steward responds with a fake-teeth smile. "No. I am a realist. I work in the system. I know the media shape and push narratives that benefit the party they back. They print the facts only when the facts help their narratives. But you, you only print the facts. Your column is *solam veritatem*. It is your pride."

"Or my conceit. What do you mean by the facts?"

"Things you can verify. But I know that you only dabble in journalism. You're really an undercover cyber hunter who for some reason likes to tell the truth, as you see it, to the public. You are known for printing inconvenient facts."

"I don't look at facts as convenient or inconvenient."

"I know, you're apolitical."

"I am not that either," Sid replies, shaking his head. "An honest journalist isn't apolitical. An apolitical person is an unthinking fool, a pawn for people like you."

He can see that Steward doesn't like that, but won't protest. Instead, the man asks him, "What is your purpose then? What is your end?"

"I know who you are, Bob Steward," Sid says, ignoring the question. "I've read your social media and your credit score and your career history and even your medical records. But I don't know *you*—your character. And I am not yet certain what your agenda is. What is it the GOP wants from me?"

Steward leans back; his chair creaks ominously, and for a moment Sid thinks it might break. Steward's eyes reveal that he thinks holding out on this bit of information is what got him this personal meeting with a man who meets few in person—and that he intends to continue holding out.

"They said you would be…but, maybe we misunderstand each other."

Bob Steward has clearly reached the end of his creative capacity.

Sid finishes the rest of his espresso and drops a twenty-dollar bill on the table. He leans in and says, barely loud enough for Bob to hear: "When you are ready to be honest, contact me again. Until then, don't waste my time."

He folds his napkin and puts it on the table.

"Please," Steward says, "let me begin again. We know you are already in this. There are emails, IP addresses, and more linking you to this dossier on the president." He reaches into his suit jacket pocket, then pushes a flash drive across the table. "I'm here to give you sources and facts about our involvement. We know you aren't so one-sided—"

"Yes, I am aware," Sid says, interrupting him, "that a group of Democrats began funding this dossier on the president when he was still just a candidate in a big primary field. I know the Republican National Committee, your team, then contracted the same Old Town Alexandria research firm, Global Positions, to continue work on the dossier after it was clear the president had secured the Democratic nomination. I know you opted not to bring it out during the election season, as it was too sensational and too poorly sourced. And I also know that it is circulating now—that someone is leaking it, and that someone has involved me. So yes, Mr. Steward: I know your fingerprints are all over this thing, and I am not yet sure where they stop."

The Republican operative is speechless for a moment, and Sid lets him sit there.

"We did fund this dossier," Steward finally says, rubbing his hands together nervously. "But all we paid for were inquiries made in public records and some interviews with foreign officials. We just wanted answers about his Russian associations, via Ukraine, and his Chinese connections. The president's family has benefited greatly from his previous positions. We know there is a lot there, but we couldn't verify enough with foreign sources to bring this to the media."

"You sound scared."

Steward straightens. The sweat sheen on his forehead catches the overhead lights.

"We had to pay people to do things, to conduct an investigation in developing nations. You know what that means. It can sound messy, even embarrassing. If it must come out, we want it to come out with the correct context."

"No one feeds me context."

"No, but..." He stops, not knowing what to say.

"If you are here because you want a scapegoat, well then, we've officially met, haven't we?"

"We are trying to help you to understand."

"No, you are here to plant information to protect your party. If that doesn't work, what then?"

"Information leaked, spun, or held is the game," Steward says, his voice wavering.

"And you are mistaking me for a player," says Sid. "You people never understand someone who isn't playing your game. I don't mean someone who breaks the rules. That's normal enough in your Machiavellian, inside-the-Beltway world. I mean someone who transcends your rules."

Steward's thick lips pucker into a befuddled expression. Sid understands; he knows the type so well he can almost read this man's mind.

To a man like Steward, someone like Sid is an impractical idealist who tries to stay above it all, up on some noble high ground—a "Mr. Smith Goes to Washington" type, who gets beaten, even destroyed, quickly and predictably by those willing to play dirty. But Sid puzzles him, because this moralist, this political outsider who always seems to have insider information, doesn't seem naive. He has something, yet he isn't looking to make a deal. Idealists are one thing; but Sid—he is something else, and that unknown something else makes him a liability.

"I know a lot now, and I will go public with it next week," Sid says.

"You're crazy!" Steward blurts, suddenly panicky. "They... they..."

"Adam will give you back your phone after I've left."

Sid stands, doesn't even glance at the flash drive on the table, and calmly walks out of the restaurant and into the moving crowd on the Fifth Avenue sidewalk.

Once around the corner, Sid steps into the back of a waiting Bentley Bentayga V8. He spreads his arms across the wide back seat as the car purrs into New York City traffic.

"Jorge, the range."

"Trouble?"

"If they're going to do it, it'll be tonight or, more likely, very early tomorrow morning. The cabin set up?"

"Just as you asked."

"You're a wonder, Jorge."

"You sure you don't want us there?"

"Quite. But I want you close."

Adam's voice comes into Sid's ear on a Bluetooth. "He took a taxi right back to Penn. Made three calls so far. Predictable—Senator Haskins, the RNC chair, and Gary Samson at Global Positions. He told them all you're going public."

"Good, send me the audio of the conversation with Samson first."

"Done."

The Midtown Tunnel flashes by, and they are in the red brick land of coffee shops and walk-ups that is gentrifying Queens.

In less than a minute, he's listening to Samson's phone call. One part, near the end, stands out.

"This man, Sidney McDaniel—I saw his shadow a few times back when I was doing financial-sector reporting for *The Wall Street Journal*. Companies, the big ones, keep this guy on retainer, but they wouldn't talk much about it. Over drinks, one financial analyst did tell me McDaniel won't work for governments. That rules out the Chinese and the Russian companies, as they are state run or controlled. He slips in, often in disguise, and always with fake names and security credentials supplied from the top, to quietly find a Chinese hack or a mole or something; he then snuffs the problem and is gone. He's a ghost and they love him for it. What he does never makes headlines, never affects their stock prices. The Street never knows he was there. I've heard he is always paid via foreign accounts from discretionary corporate funds. He doesn't want people to know how much money he has. This man is dangerous."

So said Gary Samson, the founder of Global Positions, an opposition-research firm, speaking from his company's headquarters in Alexandria, Virginia.

I'll need to meet Gary in person, but how?

The Bentley passes newly gentrified neighborhoods, then into a commercial district of nondescript warehouses. Soon they arrive at a movie and television prop company on Metropolitan Avenue.

The company specializes in training actors on the proper use of guns, as well as providing firearms experts to advise TV and movie producers and to make sure shootout scenes look realistic. The company maintains an underground firing range and an arsenal, supplying all makes and models of current and older firearms—some real, but many realistic-looking rubber replicas—whatever a TV show or movie needs in order to obey local gun laws in New York City. They also supply the fake blood, realistic disguises, and even the gore for bloody scenes in police dramas.

They've been very useful for Sid's undercover work.

"I'll be out in a few, Jorge. We're going to the cabin next."

CHAPTER 3

The cabin is located on the east side of the Shawangunk, a mountain ridge that runs north from New Jersey to just east of the Catskill Mountains in New York State. Rock climbers call it "The Gunks," and they come here to challenge its white cliffs of hard conglomerate rock.

An expanse of white and red oaks has long closed off the cabin from the homes in the Hudson Valley far below. The place was built by an eclectic architect in the late nineteenth century as an escape from New York City. It's up a long, winding, and gated driveway off a small mountain road that was cut into the rock along a natural bench on the mountainside. The surrounding forest wasn't there when the cabin was built in 1881. All this land had been logged and was mostly open. Stone walls still run everywhere in this wood, marking the boundaries of long-gone dairy farms. Photos of this area from the 1880s remind any well-traveled person of Ireland's open fields, cut by gray stone walls, dotted with cows roaming among a few sparse trees and small homes with stone chimneys.

In the 150 years since, the forest regrew into tall hardwood trees, with a canopy so thick that little else grows in the brown fallen leaves covering the shaded forest floor. The cabin, which once had a commanding view of the Hudson Valley, is now hidden in a sea of these stately trees below white cliffs.

A mountain brook, born from springs trickling from the bottom of those cliffs, falls over rocks to the cabin. It then passes over a man-made section of stream rocks cemented together, down three levels of porches to a natural swimming pool. From there it falls again—out of the pool in a thirty-foot waterfall to the natural stream bed below, before flowing fast down the steep hardwood ridge and out of sight, to the valley somewhere far down through the forest.

On summer afternoons, lying by the spring-fed pool in rays of sun filtering through green summer leaves, it is hard even to hear a car or plane beyond the barrier of oaks and maples. The brook gurgles gently, oak leaves move softly on the wind, and far below, the stream falls onto rocks rounded from eons of water pounding on them, while all about are birds, a whole forest full of them.

Sid thinks of this place as his Fortress of Solitude, though tonight it's for something else entirely. Still, he doesn't linger on that now. He has found that before going into a job, and playing some risky role with a fake name and life, he needs to let all of that fade away for a while. Comedians and politicians agree on this—that before entering the stage in front of all those people, the mind needs to be cleared so it can reset into the new scene. So he takes deep breaths and lets what's to come drift to the back of his mind. He leans back into the plush leather chair, puts his feet up, and allows his thoughts to float away, to a stream he fished the year before.

When he feels completely relaxed, he begins the motions of mental preparation, rehearsing what he has thought about and imagined himself doing. Then he stands in the darkening room and picks up a laptop computer. He leaves the high-vaulted ceiling of the cabin's living room, stooping beneath a beam split 150 years ago with an ax, and proceeds into the kitchen. In the back, he walks down creaking stairs and steps lightly onto the damp floor of the cold cellar. He clicks on a light that glows softly yellow.

The cabin's foundation is built three feet thick from the mountain's hard white conglomerate rock. It is cool and stable as a deep cave down here. He pulls on a wine rack heavy with red bottles, and it swings out as easily as a well-hung front door. Behind it is a vault door. He punches in a combination, turns a handle, pulls it open, and steps inside a safe room that's as big as a guest bedroom.

He places the laptop on a cedar shelf, alongside other hardware stashed carefully on a series of similar shelves. There are a few guns, each with a trigger lock, but none of the firearms runs afoul of New York State's Safe Act. There is some cash stacked neatly, but not more than ten thousand dollars. There is some art carefully wrapped in brown paper and then clear plastic, and he thinks again about where he'll hang the paintings that struck him in art galleries in New York. But soon he steps out and closes the vault door, then the wine rack.

He walks back up the creaky stairs as the sun sets on the other side of the mountain. He decides not to go up the hill behind the house, to the shed built into a cave in the mountainside, and turn on the generator there. Not yet. Maybe not at all tonight. Outside, twilight is turning the forest magenta, and he doesn't want to spoil the soft mood with too many lights or with a television. The energy stored from the solar panels will keep his security system going, and there is enough to run his refrigerator, a few lamps, and the water pump until morning, though he doesn't expect to be here for that long.

He bought this place because it is off the grid—a perfect escape from the undercover cyber world he spends most of his time immersed in, with its tangled web of Wall Street, politics, and international espionage. This Fortress of Solitude is a two-hour ride from that madness—just far enough to be a getaway, yet close enough for a peaceful, last-minute weekend escape.

But tonight won't stay peaceful for long.

He pours some beans into a hand grinder and enjoys the sound of turning them into grounds. He pours the grounds into a French press and lights a copper kettle on the stove. Soon, a mug of steaming coffee in his hand, he walks into the den and looks at the Frederic Church over the fireplace. He sips the coffee, then sinks into a soft, leather lounge chair next to a bay window. He puts his feet up on a leather ottoman and places the cup on a round end table. Outside the window, beyond the pool, the forest falls away into the deep purple dusk.

He is not worried. Coming here unseen is not an option—not without a lot of time, anyway. The motion detectors and cameras will give him warning. Even the long winding driveway is fitted with security cameras hidden in the forest and among the rocks, all running from solar panels placed up in the trees and cliffs. Belaying down from a helicopter is possible, but too disruptive. Besides, that would be tricky among the oaks rising over the cabin.

Sid left them one opening to avoid all of that. There is only one good vantage point for the spooks down there, and he knows the team they're likely to send will think it perfect—an ideal oversight. Downstream of the waterfall below the pool, a small dirt road meanders up from the country road a half-mile below. From a small clearing down there, a person can see up the ridge and into the windows of the kitchen and den. With the right hardware, that person could eavesdrop on Sid's off-the-grid signal, or even use a device that can pick up voices by measuring vibrations in the window glass.

Jorge assures him this kind of recon is standard procedure for any team the FBI is likely to send. While in the Green Berets, Jorge spent two years as an instructor at the U.S. Army John F. Kennedy Special Warfare Center and School at Fort Bragg. During that time, he even taught some visiting FBI agents who came in for a few weeks of training.

Sid peers out the bay window and down to that small meadow. From there it's an easy hike uphill, over the brown leaves carpeting the ground under the hardwoods, right to the cabin.

He takes his SIG 9 mm pistol out of his inside-the-waistband holster and places it on the table beside his chair. He pulls off the holster, too, and returns the pistol to it.

Then he settles back into the lounge chair, right in front of the window, opens *The Long Goodbye* to a random page, and falls comfortably into the familiar story in the waning light.

Hours pass and he has nodded off when his phone buzzes. He touches it, starting an encrypted conversation.

"They're raiding the Uptown place," says Adam. "They're taking everything. Gloria let them in after they showed her a warrant."

"You are keeping a video catalog of everything they are taking, right?"

"Just as we planned," says Adam. "Gloria is mocking them now. You should hear it."

"Good girl."

Sid hears a click and then Gloria talking; in the background, sounds of things being moved. "You sure you know how to turn that on?" she is saying. "The encryption key is a little bigger than you. When will you people ever realize you're supposed to be protecting us? Like I did during my Navy days, up in the wild blue yonder, with warheads under my wings. Down below—little blips that were targets. Clean that way. But what you're doing? Well, you're just little drones serving a Deep State and feeling so superior about it. Cheers to you and your FBI bosses, my dear friend."

"She must have a glass of wine in her hand," says Sid.

"Her favorite Chianti."

Then another voice, female, answers Gloria.

"We're just doing our duty." This woman's tone is strong, but her voice has a faint note of insecurity. As if she knows duty requires her to march right through any uncertainty, thinks Sid.

"Yes," Gloria answers, "people doing the bidding of all the governments across the world have thought and said that."

"You'll get all of this stuff back," says the woman.

"Oh? When? And who keeps all the private data? And does it get leaked? If so, or when so, what can we do about it?"

"Courts must decide all that."

"Yes, *Special Agent Baker*," Gloria replies, her voice sarcastic. "I know all the procedures and I'll file all the motions. You'll all get rebuffs from a judge later, but by then the game will have been played and started all over again—maybe in the politics of the next administration. As you are counting on."

"You're an insolent one," says the FBI agent, "but then we give you that First Amendment right."

"No," says Gloria, "that right is not from you, and it's not a gift. It's in the Constitution, and it's a restriction on government. Meaning, on the likes of you. Sadly, it's what we are losing our grip on…You're frowning, *Special Agent Baker*. I'm very sorry you don't understand that. Of all people, someone in your job should not only understand it, you should be fighting like hell for it."

Special Agent in Charge Stephanie Baker feels tired and grubby standing here in a suit she has been wearing for the past twelve hours. Strands of her blonde hair, tied up and back, have escaped and hang along her cheeks. She tugs at her wrinkled suit jacket as she carefully looks her adversary up, then down. She hates that she admires what she sees: an in-shape, confident, well-dressed, attractive woman, so sure of herself that she is comfortable lecturing the FBI agent who is leading a raid into her workplace and, indeed, into the virtual world she works within on this company's intranet, through her laptop.

Baker clears her throat. "You're not the only one here with a law degree."

"Oh? Whom did you clerk for? Where did you practice?"

"I went right into the service of my country." The woman—Gloria something-or-other—pushes her long, dark hair out of her eyes, then crosses her arms defiantly. "So you went from the legalism taught in law school to the legalism they teach in the FBI Academy. You know the rules, but not their foundation. You see the forest, but not the ground it is rooted in. Well, *Special Agent Baker*"—she emphasizes her title insultingly—"after college, I went right into the service of my country too. I flew jets for the Navy. Then I went to law school. Then I practiced. Now I am here. And you have no idea what I do. Do you?"

The woman's words and manner put her off balance. This isn't a normal feeling for her. She puts her hands on her waist, seeking reassurance from the feel of the pistol on her hip. She draws a deep breath and lets it out slowly before speaking again.

"We're not here to argue. We're here to help you…or rather, to help the American people."

"How nice. We will need a signed receipt of everything you're taking."

"Call our field office for that. We won't know what we have until it is all logged into our system."

"So, we're just supposed to trust your bureaucratic accounting?"

"You'll find we keep a good record."

"I'll bet."

"We'll also need passwords to gain access to the information in your cloud accounts."

Gloria waves her red fingernails dismissively at this. "Give me the details about these accounts you say exist, serve your warrant, and we'll comply—after a court challenge, of course."

Gloria then just smiles at Special Agent Stephanie Baker. They both know full well that the vagaries of international law will make this demand impossible to fully enforce, especially since what they are looking for are encrypted accounts moving behind VPNs between zombie IP addresses on computer networks in many other nations.

Special Agent Baker stands there a moment, wanting to say something else, to have the last word. But she can't think of anything. Angry, she turns away and goes back to looking over the rooms and giving orders to her team of agents.

Adam, sitting at a window in an apartment a block away, watches through binoculars as flashlights move in and out of the front door of the Manhattan brownstone.

He has two laptops open; each is filled with panels showing different video feeds. He uses the down arrow to flip between hidden cameras in the building. For the past hour, he has watched the FBI Enhanced SWAT team clear the house and then follow procedure to confiscate anything electronic. He hears them talking, thanks to hidden mics. After the first tense moments, they start to relax and banter openly, too freely.

Speaking into his collar mic, he says to Sid, "They're annoyed. You should hear them. They're frustrated because they are finding so little to confiscate."

"We don't keep much," Sid answers, "only what the IRS makes us maintain. And of course we store all that encrypted data on cloud networks overseas."

"This FBI team is not showing much discipline, Sid. I'm catching them talking about all sorts of things. One loves your art. She is pulling paintings off walls to look for safes or something behind them. But she is also taking pictures of the art and close-ups of the artists' names. Another can't believe how few computers, servers, or even files are in the place. He's frustrated that you don't keep any paper files or discs or something for them to grab. He is so profane, he must be from New York.... Hold on.... This Special Agent in Charge, Stephanie Baker, is on a Bluetooth phone now with someone she is calling 'Mr. Koons' or 'Kuntz' or something like that.... I'm catching most of it. She is telling him what they're finding.... *Ha*, she just picked up that Sudanese war shield of yours and called you a '*nouveau riche* tech kid with taste.'"

"That's sixteenth century elephant hide," says Sid.

"Whatever. Now two young special agents are upstairs in your walk-in closet. One is asking the other if he knows anything about you. The other thinks this is a—oh boy, he just said it's 'a political hit job ordered by the non-lifers.' I guess he means the political appointees in the Bureau.... They like your suits, Sid. One is wondering who your tailor is. He says he has seen the closets of big-time political figures, and even they don't have a wardrobe like yours."

"The English stuff is mostly from Savile Row; the Italian stuff is mostly from Rome, most of them are Brionis, but I do like Kiton, from Naples—elegant, slim-fit designs," says Sid, laughing.

"Now one—okay this one is named Jake—thinks you must be a 'stuck-up, rich shit.'"

"From the wrong side of the tracks, actually."

"This Jake says you're trying to buy your taste. He says he has seen this before. Another 'wannabe brat filled with self-importance.' He wonders why you can't 'just drop the ego trip and let those in power take care of things.'"

"These agents sure don't seem to be very focused on counterintelligence," Sid says. "And this Kuntz, he must be Neil Kuntz, chief of the FBI's Counterespionage Section. If so, he probably doesn't trust this team enough to tell them what this warrant is really about, so they are going through the motions and naturally wondering why they are raiding my home."

"Okay, now this Agent Baker is speaking to a New York newspaper reporter that the FBI invited in," Adam says. "This reporter, a Cole Thomas, is sprawled on one of your couches like he owns the place and is interviewing everyone as they pass. Let me patch through the audio, so you can hear what they are saying."

"What is it you hope to find here, Special Agent Baker?"

"That's Thomas's voice," Adam explains. "Baker is standing over him, arms crossed, looking at him like she just noticed a bug running across the carpet."

Then her voice, speaking with deliberate caution:

"Evidence of involvement with Gary Samson's team at Global Positions. Or contact with Global Position's contractors. Evidence of illegal intrusions—hacks. Maybe some contact with the Russians, but I am not sure about that. The Russians don't like direct communication. They prefer surrogates."

Special Agent Baker stops. The reporter presses for more, but she has clearly already delivered the line she was told to utter and now she just wants out of the interview.

Sid says, "Wow, they're already turning on Global Positions. Faster than I thought. I do need to meet Samson before this goes public."

"Tomorrow's edition?" says Adam.

"Maybe, but papers often sit on stories until they decide if it fits one of their narratives."

"These FBI agents are carrying anything that even looks like a computer out to a waiting van. People are watching from windows up and down the side street. It is quite the scene," says Adam.

"It's good they're taking everything. As we planned."

"I guess."

"Okay, send me the interesting stuff and see what you can find out about all of the people on this FBI team," Sid says before cutting the connection.

Sid gets up from his lounge chair, iPhone in hand. Acting casually, he looks off into the dark forest, toward where he knows that meadow is. He opens a security app and logs in. With a few movements of his fingers, he finds the right cameras and searches the meadow with an infrared lens.

He spots them there, watching him with night-vision optics. There are three of them, and they're sitting down in the clearing. One has his back resting against an oak. Another is bent over, idly plucking blades of grass. They clearly have been there a while and are bored. They are watching him and waiting for a team to gain access.

Sid puts the phone in his pocket, walks calmly into a bedroom, and places his right hand on a scanner that is on a safe mounted next to the bed. It pops open, and he places his pistol and two extra mags inside, along with his holster. He closes the safe, wishing he could carry his handgun where he is going, as he is a marked man. But his carry permit is only good for New York, and it is his secret pride that, no matter its vagaries or contradictions, he does try to follow the law to the letter. He is well aware of the ancient maxim: more law equals less justice. But he knows that, no matter how well he justifies using the loopholes in the laws, this can quickly become a rationalization, which is a slippery slope.

He walks back into the living room. While pulling on a leather jacket, his phone buzzes.

"Yes?"

"Two black SUVs are at the gate," says Jorge.

Sid has Jorge sitting in the Bentley, parked fifty feet up the driveway and facing the iron gate.

"Looks like a team is preparing to walk in. Cameras show another SUV on the road below the cabin. They're on the move too," says Jorge.

"Good. Open the gate and let them serve their warrant. Then follow them in. Make sure they don't destroy this place. If they find the safe in the basement, it should take them a while to break in."

"Oh, they'll find it," says Jorge.

"If they don't, give them a hint or two."

Jorge laughs. "The contents of that laptop should confuse them—it does me. But, you know, they can seize cash and guns."

"Yes, yes, all a part of the realism."

"Expensive props."

"Cost of doing business. Do make sure you keep a record of everything they take. Gloria will make certain the FBI gives us their records of everything of ours they are seizing or holding, as they must—but I don't trust them. Anyway, time to stir up a Deep State hornet's nest," Sid says, just before he turns off the phone.

He walks into the kitchen and opens the door that leads down a dozen stairs into the cool of the cellar. He is soon behind the foundation's three-foot-thick walls. In the complete darkness of the windowless room, he navigates by memory and feel through the basement and then reaches out for the knob of the back door. He pushes back a deadbolt and pulls open the heavy metal door. It is cold and damp and its hinges whine. He closes it behind him as he steps out into the night.

He moves on his toes up a set of stone steps that leads to a six-foot-high stone wall running along the stream that passes over the porch. He uses it for cover as he walks uphill and out of sight of any thermal imaging.

CHAPTER 4

The moon's white reflected light gives Sid's hands a ghostly look as he unlocks a fist-sized padlock on the shed built into the side of the mountain. Inside, next to the generator, is his Arc Vector motorcycle—a black, sleek, futuristic-looking bike whose designers must have been fans of the Batman movies. Sid both likes and detests this bike. He likes that it's electric, as it's quiet and has smooth power, but he hates that it's electric, as this makes it hip and politically correct—which, to him, is a populist virus. And, of course, an electric bike can be damned inconvenient, as it must be charged for forty-five minutes to be ready to go, and tonight he'll be pushing its battery to near its dead end.

The electric machine comes quietly to life, fully charged, and he rolls it out before gently closing the steel door of the shed. This bike will go from 0 to 60 mph in 2.7 seconds, but he can't do that here, on this overgrown trail in the forest. He pushes on a helmet, then lets the bike roll a mile down a forest path along the ridge, its tires lightly crunching brown leaves and dry branches, until he reaches the country road below and well past the cabin. From the road, through the trees, he can just make out the lights of the SUVs and the shadowy figures of FBI agents.

He speeds away in the moonlight. He goes a full mile before turning on the motorcycle's headlight.

The late April night has a cool humidity that feels alive on his neck, behind the collar of the leather jacket. He opens the visor on the helmet for a few miles, just to feel it on his face. He enjoys the turns on the winding country roads and feeling the bike respond. He speeds along from rural New York into Pennsylvania, then Maryland, and finally Virginia.

The sun has been up an hour when he reaches Old Town Alexandria and its quaint streets, just across the Potomac from Washington, D.C.

Old Town has the small-town feel of short buildings, quiet sidewalks, and an eclectic mix of stores opened and maintained by individuals with dreams, not just by corporate boards deciding which national chains should be included in a planned community. This has made Old Town a community everyone likes the aesthetics of, but that zoning regulations rarely allow to be naturally replicated in other parts of the country.

The town is quiet, and most of the shops are closed and dark this Tuesday morning, but he knows Gary Samson is an early starter. A background check from a discreet firm the week before found that Samson walks every weekday morning from his apartment a few blocks up to his two-story, red-brick office in a grid of coffee shops, restaurants, and bars.

At precisely 8:00 a.m. on this sunny spring morning, outside the entrance of the Global Positions building, Sid is sitting on his bike with his right leg tucked under him, watching Gary Samson, founder of

Global Positions, make his way up an uneven brick sidewalk with a Starbucks coffee in one hand and a leather briefcase in the other.

When Samson gets close, Sid says with the pleasantness of an old friend, "Good morning, Gary."

Samson stops and doesn't smile. He holds the paper Starbucks cup high in his left hand, to keep it from splashing on his blue shirt, and the leather satchel in his right. He squints at Sid but clearly doesn't recognize him and doesn't know what this is about. His office doesn't have a public address or even a sign in front.

"Don't you recognize my voice? I'm Sid McDaniel," he says as he touches a button on his side to start a video camera recording—a camera that's pretending to be a shirt button.

Samson fumbles his coffee, spilling a few drops on his blue dress shirt and red-and-blue striped tie. He looks down at the stain on his pudgy stomach and then back up at Sid.

"We need to talk, Gary."

The man glances at his office door, then back at Sid's expectant expression.

"Yes, Gary. Inside would be better."

He clearly doesn't want to go inside with Sid, but Sid gets off his bike and steps beside him. He gives in, and they go up a step to the shiny black front door of what was once a two-story brick Georgian home. Samson juggles his bag and coffee and fumbles with his keys before opening the door and leading him inside. Sid closes the front door behind them as Samson heads left, into an office with large windows facing the quiet street. The room is filled with morning light. He sets his coffee on a dark wood desk and places his bag on the floor behind it.

Sid sits in the wooden chair in front of the cluttered desk.

Samson settles his weight into a swivel chair behind it and searches Sid's face with his brown, puffy eyes. Sid offers him an expression far too empty for the man's liking.

There is an awkward silence as Samson obviously expects Sid to speak first. But Sid just looks around the room, noticing the photos with congressmen and a former president, some plaques signifying journalism awards, and a lot of books arranged for display.

"I really don't know what I can do for you," Samson says. He looks at the floor, then briefly at Sid before looking away again.

"I do."

Samson moves for his phone, but stops when Sid says, "Please keep your hands where I can see them."

"What is this?"

"An interview. Mind if I record it?"

"Um…I guess not. What do you want?"

"I want to know why you included me in that dossier on the president."

"I didn't do that," says Samson, shaking his head.

"Your sources put it together, yes?"

"Well, some of our—I mean, some sources we—"

"I've seen the communication chain," says Sid. "I know it was assembled here, as in at this IP address."

"We use a VPN."

"Not a very good one."

Samson frowns. Sid watches as the man takes in his face, leather jacket, jeans, and riding boots. He is obviously trying to understand him and figure out where this conversation is headed.

"My reputation can add authenticity, I get that," says Sid. "But I can also be a lot of trouble. More trouble than you want."

"Is that a threat?"

"No," says Sid calmly and easily, as if this were a conversation between old friends over lunch. "I just want to know what your game is."

"My game? I do investigations for clients. I source my information as best I can, but sometimes, and I tell them this, I do gather some expert opinion."

"Hearsay, gossip, innuendo—your sources are monetarily incentivized to give you fluff and hearsay, so they can earn more."

"Well," Samson says, "some will see it that way, but everything comes down to opinion, and nothing is better than expert opinion. Facts are even founded on opinion, you know—it's what weight we give them that gives facts power. And power is what drives this town."

When delivering these last words, Samson's jaw set, his eyes hardened, and conviction seemed to fill him up, like hot air expanding a balloon.

"These experts you use don't even have to put their names behind their opinions, as you cloak their identities."

"Well, since these are often former intelligence agency professionals, I could hardly attach their names to these documents."

"No skin in the game for them, yet you act as if their information were solid."

"What is solid? This desk isn't even solid. I could bust it up with a good hammer," says Gary, shrugging.

"Oh, I see—everything is relative."

"No, not everything." Samson lets out a big breath in exasperation. "Death is hardly a relative notion, but most things are. Right now, outside, it is sunny and sixty degrees, according to my thermometer right there." He points out a window, but Sid doesn't look. "Those are facts, but they are hardly absolutes. The humidity that people feel is another fact, but people feel it differently. The wind speed, whether the sun is out or not, those are facts too, but they are subject to perceptions that people react to differently, even feel differently. And anyway, in the time I take to communicate the facts, perhaps a cloud passes between us. Facts, you see, are hardly steady things. What matters is the *narrative* we apply, because the facts are ever-changing and up to interpretation."

"You sound like the Washington media."

"I was a journalist."

"Yes, and quite the education you've had," says Sid. "Do you think values change so easily, or are they, perhaps, steadier things?"

"*Values?*" asks Samson mockingly. "They are *always* up to interpretation, subject to the whims of people, to their rationalizations, and they rely on the context of any given event—Just ask any trial lawyer who has dealt with a few juries. Just ask any politician who has won an election. Voters will forgive almost anything if someone is on their team. Most things are relative."

"I see, there is no right and wrong—just the narrative and whatever power some version of an evolving story can bring you. That's a very convenient philosophy."

Sid glances around the cluttered office of a man who researches political figures for a living. Amid the photos and mementos are piles of newspapers, shelves of books from the elites of the Washington political establishment, and a set of scrubby golf clubs in a corner.

"There is some legal guidance, I suppose," says Samson, "but even that shifts with Supreme Court precedents as political power nominates and installs justices."

Sid smiles and comfortably lets another long, awkward pause settle over the room before finally speaking again. "Still, despite your open view of the facts, traces of me are in the metadata of that dossier, and I was included as a 'source'—and that isn't a matter of ever-changing interpretation. This *fact* is now being leaked. It is being leaked to the media that I had something to do with this 'Dirty Document' on the president that your team put together. Now, we did speak once, about a year ago, in an encrypted, off-the-record conversation. That conversation was about a banking client we then both shared. I spoke to you because the client asked me to. I tried to help you, and maybe I did. But that had nothing to do with this latest op-research document on our president."

Samson shrugs again. "Actually, the president had various accounts with that bank. And he had wire transfers from that bank to various other accounts that have established connections to the Kremlin and to the Chinese government. And so it *does* fit into this, very neatly. The president's family also used that bank, and some of their transfers are very questionable. In fact, many of your investigations were useful to this dossier and, from what I've been told, you even sent us information via encrypted dummy accounts. Your work is, in many ways, all through it. So there *is* an association, isn't there?"

"I see. Back to those pliable facts in the twisted digital narrative you shape, or try to," says Sid. "And the metadata?"

"Do I look like a computer geek to you?"

"It's not in your resumé, but a few of the firms you hire are capable of this. Some have intricate NSA connections, since certain high-profile and former administration people have moved from the intelligence agency to jobs in those K Street firms."

"Oh, that sounds so conspiratorial," he responds, mocking. Clearly he has his feet back under him. "There is more. You had contact with some of my researchers. A few of your cases—ah, some of the contract jobs you did for various companies—were also a big help. Some of that was supplied by third parties, but your hands are all over it."

Sid almost laughs at the absurdity of all this. "I have contact with a lot of people. Some are powerful; some are informants; some are people I meet while I am undercover, and so are playing a part in my investigations. I do come into contact with a lot of shady people." Sid pauses, leaning in. "But I don't work for governments, and I've never looked into this president or had anything to do with assembling this opposition-research document."

"Murky isn't it?" Samson responds, his voice now light-hearted. "So small a world at the top. The heads of the companies you work for give money to political parties and rub elbows with them, and around them orbit all sorts of other characters who are attracted to their power and money." He shakes his head. "You are dirtier than you think, Sid McDaniel."

"I see," says Sid. "So, I am dirty because I enter the system to clean out bad actors. As dirty as a good cop who spends his days in the worst neighborhoods."

Samson chuckles. "You really do see yourself as a good guy. I wasn't sure before, but that's it, isn't it? You have delusions of grandiosity."

Sid shrugs. "I try to follow a code, to stay clean, but I am human. As for you, though, you're in deep this time, Gary. These Deep State people see you as expendable. They are playing a game for all the marbles, while all you want is to get paid well by either party."

Samson's eyes search Sid's. "What are you getting at?"

"Thunder is on the horizon, my morally relativistic friend. This storm is about to get loud, very loud, and you'll be caught in the middle of it. In fact, they are already leaking your involvement."

Sid pulls the iPhone from a pocket, opens the Utilities app, and plays a clip of a recording:

"What is it you hope to find here, Agent Baker?"

"Evidence of involvement with Gary Samson's team at Global Positions. Or contact with Global Position's contractors. Evidence of illegal intrusions—hacks. Maybe some contact with the Russians, but I am not sure about that. The Russians don't like direct communication.

They prefer surrogates." The little audio clip ends. Sid looks Samson in the eyes and says, "That was FBI Special Agent Stephanie Baker talking to a New York newspaper reporter last night."

"What?" Samson's voice jumps. He quickly attempts to hide the reaction with a toss of his head and a nervous laugh.

Sid leans in closer and continues. "I already know about the retired British spy you had gather information for you. I know about his source: a Ukrainian-born Russian who worked in this town for a think tank. A Russian with known connections to the Kremlin, who has since fled the country. This is damning stuff. The Chinese stuff is even worse. You even gave payoffs to corrupt officials."

"It's not like that!" Samson shouts.

"If you'll fill me in with some details on your clients—who they are and what they wanted from you—I can make this a lot less painful," says Sid. "Often, people hide behind lawyers and lie and plead the Fifth, when the better play is to be forthright and then move on."

After a few seconds, Samson rallies, and his laugh almost sounds genuine. "You're such a computer geek, McDaniel. No, worse—you're a New Yorker used to the ways of the financial district. You speak plainly, as only New Yorkers can, and I like that. But this isn't math, or even the simple fear and greed that drives the market. This isn't what you're used to in the cyber world or on the Street. This is Washington, my friend; this is hardball politics. The truth doesn't matter here. As I said, only the narrative matters, as shaped by those in power. That includes those in government, but also the money people in politics, and the media who play the game. I can hear the storm coming, sure. But it isn't coming for me. I'm useful. I'm a team player on the winning team. You? You're expendable. You're exposed. I have dirt on them. You have, what? Self-righteousness?"

"Yes, dirt—you have that. But you're partly buried already, and you don't even know it."

Samson scowls and says, "You are the one they want."

"Why?"

"Your involvement is a good distraction, I suppose," Samson says arrogantly. Then his face flushes, as Sid sees him realize he said more than he wanted to say.

Sid asks, "So, who are 'they'?"

Samson just shakes his head.

"Senator Haskins—you know, the chairman of the Intelligence Committee—is beginning to ask questions, Gary."

"That arrogant fool?"

Sid doesn't like the snarl that just flashed on Samson's face before it was quickly suppressed. For an instant, something tried to get out. Something angry. Something scared.

"What scares you," Sid says as he focuses hard into the black holes of the man's pupils, "is that, deep down, you know I am not selling a false narrative. I am telling a true story, and I already know a lot. Despite your elastic view of facts, the truth has a way of resonating when it gets out. But though you are clearly scared of the truth, you think I'm naive to believe I can bring the truth to the public in a way that'll unravel whatever phony narrative comes from you or your anonymous government sources."

"And then some."

"Then why do bureaucrats always scurry like roaches when the light comes on? Why are they so scared whenever an honest whistleblower comes forward?"

"You need to grow up. Whistleblowers have agendas too," says Samson. But his words sound tentative, and his face flushes slightly.

Sid smiles his easy smile and says, "I think you forgot something."

"What?"

"I said this was an interview."

Samson stands so fast his stomach scrapes on his desk, making his red-and-blue striped tie stretch and bounce. He glares at Sid.

"That's right, Gary. Remember? You didn't ask me to keep this off the record."

Samson moves to step around the desk, but stops himself. He clenches his fists helplessly.

"At least that was an honest reaction," Sid says. He stands, turns, and walks out into the morning sun.

Leaving the remote-listening device on the floor, just under Gary Samson's desk, was as simple as dropping it down a pantleg. The device costs $79.95 and can be bought from dozens of stores. Linking its app to a throwaway phone was easy too.

Bugging Gary's office is illegal, and Sid does not like breaking laws. Bend them, sure; find the holes in them, of course; but never break them. Sid thinks that ordinary people who break laws to get what they want are the fools of the system. They are risking everything. By contrast, the white shirts of Wall Street and Washington bend the rules and make fortunes all the time, and they are rarely held accountable: even when caught, tried, and convicted, they get deals or simply retire comfortably.

So, this cheap bit of illegal eavesdropping does bother Sid, but it is not traceable—well, not as long as he soon tosses the burner phone in the Potomac River.

Sid gets on his motorcycle and listens in on Gary cursing. He hears pounding that he assumes is Gary slamming his fist on his desk. He hears Gary pick up and put down his coffee cup as he mutters profanity. As he rides away, he hears Gary take deep breaths;

then there are the short beeps of numbers being tapped into a cell phone.

"Yeah, it's me.... He was here.... Yes, Sid McDaniel was here.... Yes, yes, I'm using the phone you gave me.... I don't know, he wanted to know about my clients.... No, of course I haven't leaked this thing to anyone. You want it quiet, so I buried it. You know I just want this to go away too.... Of course I didn't tell him anything!....The question is what are *you* going to do?.... That's not enough. I'm exposed—exposed, and you're leaking my fucking involvement!.... Then who is?.... Neil, he played me a recording of one of your agents, ah, Baker, leaking my name to the papers. So just what kind of game are you playing?.... I know about that, and I know our involvement going public is inevitable, but not like this—not right at the beginning. We're supposed to be an asterisk, not the main storyline.... Can't you arrest him or something?.... Yeah, I'll calm down.... I do need you to do something. He said he was going to quote me.... Oh, no—nothing big, I don't know, I said some things about my methods, but nothing particular. I did say it won't stick to me.... Does he have audio? I'm assuming he does.... Okay, thanks Neil.... Oh shit, right, I'm sorry. I'm just a little upset.... Did I what?.... Did I sweep my office?"

Sid hears a chair roll back and feet on hardwood, and then, "Oh shit."

Sid grins.

He pulls up next to what's known as the old Torpedo Factory and walks to the river alongside a seafood restaurant. He looks around and, seeing no one watching, tosses the phone out into the water. He then calls Adam on another temporary phone, after first logging in through an encryption app.

"Gary was just speaking to a Neil. Could it be Neil Kuntz, chief of the FBI's Counterespionage Section?"

"That's who this Special Agent Baker was speaking to last night," says Adam.

"Okay, keep digging, but be careful. Stay behind those proxy servers. Also, I need everything on FBI Special Agent Stephanie Baker, especially her chain of command."

"No need to tell me that sort of thing. It's well under way. Jorge is local. I'll be on the Acela."

"Good. And yeah, I guess I am a little worked up."

Sid calls Jorge.

"You watching Gary Samson?"

"Yes, and I am bringing in freelancers."

"That former SEAL and his little team of Florida derelicts?"

"Yes."

"And I thought Green Berets and SEALs didn't mix," says Sid, laughing.

"He's good, and he's tired of surveilling cheating husbands and gambling housewives. We could use the backup. He is a little expensive for this sort of gig."

"Whatever it is, it's worth it."

"By the way," says Jorge, "those FBI agents were pretty fucking mad that you slipped out of the cabin. They threatened to arrest me if I didn't tell them where you were hiding. I held out my hands for the cuffs, and they basically told me to fuck off. A lot of what they said was picked up by the security system—they were too mad for discipline. They clearly wanted to interrogate you on the record and in the heat of the moment, even though they didn't have an arrest warrant, just the search warrant. Anyway, as I said, the security system recorded all of it. You can log in any time to hear it."

"They do like perjury traps," Sid says. "If you just give a different anecdote, or try to explain something in greater detail on a second interview, which are normal things to do, then they've got you in a possible felony."

"Get a few hours of rest," says Jorge. "I'm texting you an address of a townhome. It has a garage, so you can plug in your cute electric bike. It's in Arlington, rented under Simon Templar."

"The Saint?"

"Seemed appropriate."

The little windowless office sits beneath the U.S. Capitol Building. Sid had heard that senators with enough seniority get these secondary offices, where they can wait for votes up on the floor. To get here on this Tuesday afternoon, he first had to meet Senator Rich Haskins's chief of staff in the Russell Senate Office Building, then go downstairs with her to take an underground train that only Members, staff, and guests can ride to the Capitol Building.

From there it was a short walk to this private basement office. The ceiling is low, and ductwork takes over part of the room, but it is clean, and it has a desk and chairs, and there are fewer eyes down here to see them together.

Sid is wearing a suit for this meeting, but he left off the tie. The suit is blue, the kind of blue only Brioni can do. He happens to like the garnish of cufflinks, which he has used to add some bright silver to the suit. He has a folded white linen handkerchief in his breast pocket and a pinhole camera peeping through its white fabric. His shoes are brown Oxfords. He regrets not shaving for the past three mornings, which has given him the fashionably unshaven look popular in the Style section of the *Times*, but which doesn't feel right for a meeting with a senator. He is thankful Jorge got down in the Bentley with his suits and other uniforms for battle.

Carole, the chief of staff, is maybe thirty, unmarried if her ring finger is honest, and has that Midwestern manner that somehow manages to belie her own good looks, which she tries unsuccessfully to minimize in a square-fitting skirt, blouse, and jacket. The senator she works for is from Iowa, and so is she: a small-town Iowa girl making it big in Washington, D.C., but getting to the age when she is wondering what's next.

"Have you met the senator before?" she asks.

"No."

"He is so eager to meet you, but I don't know who you are."

"I'm just a man."

She smiles. His comment was designed to smother the possibility of getting to the personal, but he does want to speak with her.

"What town in Iowa are you from?"

"Albia. It's so small. You know, one of those little Midwestern places with a town square that could have been the set for *Back to the Future*—movie theatre, clock over the town hall, and all," she says, her eyes flirting and her body leaning forward.

The door opens before Sid can reply, which disappoints him. In comes Senator Richard Haskins wearing his politician smile. The senator is small, maybe five foot six, and slight and elderly, but his eyes are glowing with life. His suit is well worn and old-fashioned. He has a white linen handkerchief in his lapel pocket and gold cufflinks on his custom-tailored sleeves.

Sid stands and shakes the senator's hand.

"I hope Carole has taken care of you. Coffee or water?"

"Oh, sorry, I didn't even offer," Carole says, blushing.

"No, thank you," says Sid, taking a chair as the senator moves behind his desk and sits. Once comfortable, he smiles and leans forward on his elbows.

"So, you're wondering about the Whistleblower Protection Act."

"I admire your directness, Senator."

"Well, I have but a minute before we vote again. Procedural stuff today, but it's necessary. It won't give you any protection, you know—not that whistleblowers are ever really protected from the federal bureaucracy. Even senators can't do much to help them; we can just send letters and say things to cameras and threaten meaningless contempt proceedings. Even the Intelligence Community Whistleblower Protection Act of 1998 is useless for you. You were never a federal contractor, not according to the intelligence briefings I've been given."

"Yes, I was careful not to be."

"The Intelligence Community Whistleblower Protection Act is full of holes anyway. National security whistleblowers don't even have court access to challenge retaliation. Actually, the whole damn system is internal. Congressional intelligence committees can intervene to help protect a whistleblower, in theory anyway, but a whistleblower can't even come to me until they've spoken to their agency's inspector general—a politically appointed character who will almost always shut the person down and set them up to be sidelined or fired for speaking up."

"Yes, I understand that the intelligence community has written all of this legislation, and I did say I wanted to talk about that. But it was only pretense," Sid says. "I wanted to get your measure, as I'll want to reach out with more actionable stuff when the time comes."

"Oh?"

"And it's coming soon—days, maybe hours."

"And you think I'll help," Senator Haskins says, leaning back into his chair with a look that says he doesn't know if he will.

"Yes, as it'll be in your interest."

"Oh?" The senator holds Sid's eyes.

"You like sending public letters seeking accountability. You like sunlight. It is why you wrote the Whistleblower Protection Act. It is what your voters expect of you."

"Rewrote."

"Right," says Sid. "An investigation will be necessary. Hearings, Senator."

"On?"

"Why, the latest Deep State coverup, of course."

"Gloria, how is the office?"

Sid sits on his bike in the rosy glow of a soon-to-set sun. He's parked on a quiet side street stacked with cute three-story townhomes painted in pleasing pale hues.

"We just swept and found only a couple of bugs," says Gloria. He pictures her at her desk in front of a new laptop, on the second floor of the Manhattan office. "Makes me wonder if we missed some roach listening to us from the dark of a heating duct or something."

"Some of their better equipment does turn on and off, so you have to sweep multiple times and check everywhere," says Sid. "What shape is the office in?"

"They took all the hardware. They came in here with an enhanced FBI SWAT team. It's all on the security cameras. You should see their outfits. Full tactical gear. Wanted to intimidate us or something. One even had a Remington Model 700 sniper rifle with a NightForce scope. Anyway, they're flipping mad that all the computers had just come from a rental company. One of those Department of Justice lawyers just called to demand the 'real stuff,' as if we are that old-fashioned. He threatened us with more subpoenas. I guess they can come and get my latest laptop. I hope not. I just refreshed it with some contacts from one of the cloud accounts."

"Did you get this attorney's contact info?"

"Yes, a Steve Jacobs. Washington, D.C., office bureaucrat. I'll send you a file on him now."

"They might just come back. No doubt they have a FISA Court warrant to eavesdrop."

"Yes. Can they get into these phones?"

"Sure, via the cell signal. The encryption will take them time, which is why we change the keys and burners so often."

"By the way," says Gloria, "Jorge says they weren't kind to your cabin. The FBI SWAT team up there ripped the vault door right off with some kind of controlled-explosive device. They seized everything in there, even the stuff behind the false wall in the safe. They had some kind of a scanning device."

"Well, good for them."

"Sometimes I think you're too nonchalant about all of this, Sidney. These guys are playing for real, you know."

"Never care about the possessions," says Sid, "just the people. And always keep the capital fluid and diversified so they can never get it all. Do that and you too will be relaxed about this sort of thing."

"I call bullshit on that, Sidney. I've seen how you care about some of those old relics of yours—the bamboo fly rods, those things from your mother, and the letters from, what is her name? Oh, Aster. And the rest of that stuff you keep secreted away."

"Any threat of an arrest warrant?" Sid answers, ignoring her comment. "I need to know how long I can move openly."

"Could be anytime," Gloria says, purposely using a bored tone in a failing attempt to rile him. "All they'll need to do is go to their rubber-stamp judge for the warrant."

CHAPTER 5

That Tuesday evening, Mack Davis, opinion editor of the *New York Herald*, is losing his cool, something Sid knows he usually does only when alcohol and a young woman are involved.

"You just want me to publish this?"

"Yes, Mack, online in the wee hours and in the morning edition," says Sid into a headset as he maneuvers his bike in Washington traffic on his way across the Potomac and into Virginia.

"Has your lawyer even seen this?"

"She helped me write it."

"Does she like you very much? It's all over the news that they tossed your Uptown place. The damn FBI invited the reporters in and just let them sit there on your nice white couches and ask questions. Your upstate place is news, but so what? As for this interview with Gary Samson at Global Positions and these details on how someone apparently faked your involvement in this 'Dirty Document,' no one knows about it yet, and besides, it's all too technical. Readers won't follow you."

"Are you worried about being sued?" Sid asks as he parks in a quiet cul-de-sac amidst rows of Arlington townhomes.

"No. You seem to have covered yourself. You gave me the audio of Samson and all that audio of those agents talking in your Uptown place. You also gave me links to tons of code I can't comprehend on the metadata, which, I guess, proves your innocence—I have a computer forensic firm looking at it and the other data you sent. You explain that part of it well enough, but there is too much here all stuffed into eight hundred words. This isn't a column, Sid; it's CliffsNotes."

"Mack, you taught me how to create a multi-part narrative. Every sentence there is designed to lead to something else. Some of it is inside baseball stuff, fine. Those links to the code are there to keep the NSA busy as much as they are to confuse the media. Every sentence in this op-ed is there to stir them up. Look, I'm playing fast chess here, and they think it's checkers. I need to keep ahead of them. Anyway, everything is factual, and it'll also leave the reader wanting more, a lot more—I know you like that. And I'll have much more soon."

"When?"

"Soon," says Sid as he sits on his bike in the evening light.

"When?"

"Maybe tomorrow, if you run this."

"And if I don't?"

"I'll find a new publisher."

"Who, Project Veritas?"

"If that's what it'll take," says Sid. "Look Mack, things are moving fast now, and I am all in, thanks to them. I'm not going to let the news cycle eat me. I am going to feed it *them*."

At 7:00 p.m., Special Agent Stephanie Baker pulls up to her townhome on a tree-lined street just a mile from the Pentagon in

Arlington. As her garage door opens, she sees in her peripheral vision someone waving to get her attention. She turns and notices Sid McDaniel on the seat of his black motorcycle with his black helmet off. He is parked on the curb under a flowering crab apple tree. He is wearing jeans and a black leather jacket and is seated with one leg crossed over the bike's black seat.

She turns off her car and steps out, but keeps the door open and her body between her black Maserati GranTurismo and McDaniel. She places her right hand on the pistol in the outside-the-waistband holster behind her suit jacket while watching Sid's hands and scanning for other threats to her sides.

"I'd like to speak with you, Special Agent Baker," says Sid without moving.

"About?"

"I'd like to check the accuracy of a quote. Well, not the accuracy, as I have audio of you, but I'd like to find out what you meant by it."

"You're playing journalist today?"

"It is one of my hats."

◈

She frowns. Sid realizes she is a very attractive woman. With her hair down, and wearing something more becoming than drab loose slacks and a coat, well, she would be striking.

"But there is no special right for the media in this country," Sid continues, trying to get her to talk a little. "We all have the same First Amendment rights. If the government ever tried to license the media, as they do in many other nations, any honest court would strike down the attempt on First Amendment grounds. Government officials can control some media access, but not who can write or speak. So, this really isn't such a different role for me."

"I know you write some opinion, but—"

"Oh, I wasn't aware there is a difference between opinion and news in the media today."

She actually smiles at this. "Regardless, all media requests to the FBI must go through our media relations."

"Yes, I've called them. Very polite people. And they are getting back to me—they even forwarded me to a department that gave me a receipt for the pistol one of your teams took from my cabin. But I am here because I wanted to get more of a sense of you. I heard everything you said in my New York City place and, of course, everything that was said in my upstate cabin, but I wanted to see something for myself."

Her eyes widen. "How did you—"

"A live connection—I'm not going to tell you the rest."

She squares up her body, stares, and demands: "What do you mean by seeing *something* for yourself?"

"You don't look at all like I expected. Your social media never shows you, except the college track stuff, the friends who've shown pictures of you, and the high school yearbook stuff and all the rest—well, you look like much more."

"Than what?" Her eyes tighten and her tone sharpens. Sid realizes she doesn't like this. She is used to questioning people like him as they sit with charges hanging precariously over their heads.

"Than how you presented yourself to my attorney," he replies, his tone sharpening when it hit "attorney."

Sid puts an earbud from his iPhone in his ear and touches the phone to start a recording. He then repeats what he hears: "You said: 'U.S. Attorneys don't play politics. When they obtain a warrant, it is for good reason. But as you'll see, this warrant isn't just for Sidney McDaniel. It is for his entire organization, and that includes you and everything in this residence. This firm is guilty, ma'am; we just don't know what you're guilty of yet.'

He tugs out the earbud. "I like that you called my attorney 'ma'am,'" he says, "but I am confused. Were you just on a fishing expedition, Agent Baker, searching for a crime, knowing everyone has broken some law or regulation—or were you there trying to gather evidence for a reported crime? Warrants, as you must know since you have a law degree, can't be issued without 'probable cause,' thanks to our Fourth Amendment protections."

Agent Baker's eyes narrow further, all the way into a Dirty Harry stare. Keeping her right hand near her holster, she pulls out her phone with her left, taps a number in her contact list with her thumb, and raises it to her ear.

"I hoped we could talk," Sid says with a shrug, genuinely disappointed, "but then all I really wanted was to get a sense of you."

Watching him carefully, she says into the phone, "I'm speaking to Sidney McDaniel right now. No, not on another line. He is here, outside my place."

Sid pushes his black motorcycle helmet on and reaches into his jacket pocket for his gloves.

She pulls out her pistol and points it at him.

He stops moving. "A Glock? I thought you people all carried SIG's these days."

She is whispering into her phone, but he sees her mouth ask, "What should I do?"

He laughs. "Agent Baker, I was just reaching for my gloves. May I show you?"

"Left hand," she says. "Very slowly."

He complies, then waves his gloves. "See? So—Am I under arrest?"

She lowers her gun, but doesn't holster it. "No, not yet."

"Still checkers, *huh*?"

"What?"

Sid pulls his helmet back off and says, "I've emailed you a copy of a column that quotes you—you said a lot that night in my home. If you object to that, I'll remind you that my attorney—you remember Gloria—informed you that you were being recorded, per the law. If you respond tonight before 10:00 p.m., or the FBI's media relations does, I should be able to add something to the piece—if, that is, you or the FBI want to add some clarification."

She loses her poker face as her eyes search his and her lips tighten.

Suddenly he wonders, for just a moment, what a man would have to do to romance a woman like FBI Special Agent Stephanie Baker. He knows she is thirty years old, athletic and strong, but still feminine, despite her lack of makeup and the suit she's chosen to hide her figure. Being strong and feminine are hardly in contradiction, he thinks, but so few American women are willing or able or maybe have the confidence to be the strong *femme fatale* or a feminine heroine when they take on traditionally masculine roles. A shame, because they relinquish an important part of their potential power to the mediocrity of political correctness.

But this Agent Baker pulls it off as well as he has ever seen. Not showy, but not starchy either. It is as if she is attractive but doesn't know it, which is the most alluring thing of all. All of this makes it even more worth the effort to knock her off balance.

"I have nothing to confirm or deny," she says as her face hardens into edges of granite and her eyes become cold blue crystals. She returns her Glock to its holster.

Sid shrugs but keeps eye contact with Agent Baker, now standing straight and statuesque under the yellow streetlights. He is genuinely sad that he must move on. He pushes his helmet on again and slips on his gloves. Raising his right palm, he smiles and nods goodbye, as an old friend might.

Then he lets the bike take him around the end of the cul-de-sac and out onto Army Navy Drive.

CHAPTER

6

"Your Global Positions guy, Gary Samson, is in Shelly's Back Room, over on F Street—two blocks from the White House," Sid hears Jorge say into his helmet's Bluetooth as he rides with the red light of a sunset on him.

"He is sitting with someone we haven't yet identified. The facial-recognition software has a few matches on Facebook and Instagram. Give me a moment to look through to see if I can ID him."

"Where in the restaurant are they?"

"They are speaking in the back. Adam's pinhole camera is catching them whenever he turns to relight his cigar."

Sid takes the Fourteenth Street Bridge over the Potomac River into Washington. Traffic is light in the evening as he comes into town. He accelerates and maneuvers easily between red taxis and Uber drivers without drawing too much attention to himself.

"Do you have audio?" Sid says into a Bluetooth linked to one of his phones as he drives.

"Adam does. He is smoking a cigar in one of the leather chairs along the wall right next to them, and they are acting like he isn't even there."

"Yeah, that's Washington. Officials have so many meetings in restaurants and bars on the Hill they just get casual about it."

"I'm linking the live audio to your phone now," says Jorge.

Sid hears someone say, "Calm down, Gary. We have to be patient. You can't lose your cool with these guys."

Sid pulls into an underground garage beneath Shelly's and takes a ticket. He parks the bike in a tiny spot between compact cars and cables his helmet to the frame of the bike.

"I'm below in the garage. Be there in a minute," says Sid as he listens to a live feed from Adam's surveillance equipment.

There is bar background noise inside Shelly's, but also remarkably clear audio of Gary Samson and this other man speaking.

"This has to be managed. They want this to go away, but how? It has been widely leaked," says Samson in urgent whispers.

"It is getting out of control," agrees the other man.

"He says he is going with articles—his damned little column. This guy never should have been yanked into this," Samson says.

"I have not been briefed on how or why that happened," says the other man.

"He came to see me. He is moving freely around town. He even saw Senator Haskins. He is getting somewhere. And he does have the document. So, what can be done? You must have stuff on him from what you gathered in the raids. We have to let Neil and the others know we won't stand for this."

Jorge breaks into the feed to whisper in Sid's ear. "Okay, the other guy is DOJ. It's the U.S. Attorney, Steve Jacobs. The same goon who called Gloria, as if she is an attorney they can rattle."

Steve Jacobs, meanwhile, is starting to regret meeting with Samson. After all, he is a U.S. Attorney, whereas this Gary Samson guy just runs a temporarily convenient opposition-research firm. Samson has a little power, as he knows things about his clients from both parties, but he has no *real* power, since he'd destroy his reputation and company if he ever dared use any of that low-grade dirt. Given this, Jacobs isn't even going to consider pushing back against the FBI leadership for the sake of Gary Samson.

"They don't want to arrest him. They have some reason, but they won't tell me," Steve says with a distant tone ending with a sigh.

"Don't you have *anything* on McDaniel?"

"Not much. This one is careful. Everything is encrypted and stored on foreign networks. He doesn't keep files, at least not any we've found. There is some video footage of clients hiring him that we seized from corporations, but all that does is expose those companies to little things—corporate slush funds and such. Many of the people at these Wall Street firms are Democratic donors," says Jacobs, sighing again.

Hearing this, Sid stops walking and says, "Okay, let me log in to read Jacobs's bio." He leans against a building on a sidewalk busy with people in suits going home or for dinner and drinks.

"I see," says Sid, scrolling down the screen. "George Mason for undergrad and law. He clerked for a circuit court judge, a Democratic appointee. Then government jobs. No big cases I can see. Married, two teenage children now in prep schools. Social media is boring. An elitist. Smug. Unoriginal. A perfect tool."

Jorge, parked in the Bentley just up the street, is laughing. "I'll bet an FBI profiler found him, felt him out, and recruited him all in one day. Jacobs was on several legal teams in the previous administration. He did research to defend various executive actions. He was also on a DOJ team to place gag orders on some journalists that the administration spied on. Clever stuff from a bureaucrat's point of view. To get out of the gag orders, the journalists had to prove harm—but they couldn't do that without first getting evidence from the intel community, which of course blocks all such attempts on national security grounds. Round and round it goes."

Sid nods to himself. "I see. Just another political player in the Deep State game—not a queen, maybe a bishop, perhaps only a pawn. I'll have to prod him a little to see if he's a robot or a thinking man."

"Sounds like they're about to break up their little off-the-record meeting."

"Okay, I'm going in."

Sid walks in the front door of Shelly's and moves to the back. He passes couches half-filled with people in suits sipping drinks and talking, enjoying the clubby atmosphere of the popular watering hole for Washington's elite. As Sid gets close, Adam quietly gets up, turns away, and walks right by him, on his way to the bar across the room, without even glancing at Sid. Sid takes Adam's leather chair along the wall and right next to Gary Samson and Steve Jacobs. Neither notice him. They are both looking at each other, oblivious to all the people moving around them for the thirty minutes they've been there.

Sid steals a glance. Jacobs is a late-middle-aged man who has worn a Brooks Brothers suit for so many years he hasn't unbuttoned his collar, loosened his tie, or even taken his jacket off, but only habitually unbuttoned it when he sat down for an after-hours drink following a full day in the controlled climate of an office.

A waitress stops in front of Sid, and he says clearly, with a slight over-projection of his voice: "Sherry. The Tio Pepe Palomino Fino would be grand."

Samson, seated on the other side of the small dark cocktail table to Sid's left, has to turn his whole chubby body to look over his right shoulder at Sid. When their eyes meet, Samson's lips try to retreat into his mouth as his eyes pop out like a carp's.

"Why hello, Gary," says Sid before looking past him and adding: "And you must be Steve Jacobs."

Jacobs's eyebrows jump behind round eyeglasses. It's obvious that he recognizes Sid, who smiles at his reaction. *I bet that in his twenty years as a U.S. Attorney, he has never seen or even heard of such theatrics from a person under active investigation.*

"Steve, this is Sid McDaniel," says Samson, in the under-the-breath way people use to broadcast genuine disdain.

"Yes, yes, I know," Jacobs says, quickly recovering and shifting into an almost pleasant tone. He is startled, but also in a strange way delighted. He is not sure why. Perhaps it's the excitement of being in a secret meeting with a man under investigation for multiple felonies. The situation intrigues him. It's like a scene out of a classic film noir, a scene just before someone gets splattered with a Tommy gun. Or maybe it's a James Bond film, and he is now meeting the super villain. Yes, he likes that allusion better. It means he is smart and classy enough to speak with the super villain and to walk away clean.

"Gary and I spoke yesterday, but I wanted to meet you in person," says McDaniel, looking past Gary into his eyes.

Jacobs nods, but doesn't get up. He isn't sure what to do. Puzzled, he finally asks, "Why?"

"To get a sense of you. It is, after all, difficult to play chess blind."

"Chess?"

"And your king is in danger," says McDaniel.

"My king?"

"Steve, we need to leave," says Gary.

Jacobs looks at Gary, but then back at McDaniel. He is quickly losing the humor that two scotch-and-sodas and the intrigue of this not-so-clandestine meeting have given him.

"What's your interest in me?" McDaniel asks him pleasantly as a waitress sets a glass of sherry beside him and moves away.

Jacobs now leans forward to look past Gary so he can better inspect McDaniel. The question is what he'd expect from someone under investigation. With his eyes searching McDaniel's, he says, "That document is filled with legally suspect material, including material obtained by hacks, illegal wiretaps, and paid foreign sources who work for foreign governments. And let's not even get into the possible collusion of a campaign with a foreign government to attain that hacked information—that's a play we've seen before. I wouldn't do anything with it, if I were you. It'll eat you up."

Gary pulls his stomach up out of the chair with his arms, gets his balance, turns and says, "Steve, I advise you to leave now."

"In a minute. This character interests me. You know, McDaniel, you're not what I expected."

"Oh?"

"You are much younger and so, well, so calm."

McDaniel's eyes soften into amusement.

"Yes, and I did imagine you to be less congenial," says Jacobs. "Maybe more strident and unsophisticated. Maybe, ah, something like a man-child living in his parents' basement—a pasty sort who spends all day and night in the soft light of a computer screen."

Now McDaniel genuinely smiles. "Can I get you another drink, Mr. Jacobs?"

"Steve," says Gary, still standing there, fat and awkward.

"No, two is my limit."

"What do you plan to do with me?" asks McDaniel.

"Can't say."

"Do you think you have much of a case?"

"That is a certainty," says Jacobs, taking off his glasses and wiping them with a cloth from his suit's breast pocket.

"That's Neil Kuntz's assessment?"

"Oh, him?" Jacobs puts his glasses back on. "Well, yes, but—"

"Steve!"

"Oh, okay, Gary." He turns back to McDaniel. "He is right. I am just an attorney, not a field person. And this is really improper."

"Oh, I don't know. I think a man should be able to meet those who are trying to frame him."

"Frame? No. We're finding plenty of things on you."

"Such as that I was falsely included as a source for this 'Dirty Document' that Samson's team assembled?" McDaniel nods at Gary.

"We did no such thing. We are simply investigating," says the DOJ lawyer.

"I can show how the data was altered," McDaniel says. "The tools used are from the kit the U.S. government developed—likely this was done by the NSA. That'll be in my column in the morning."

"I doubt you can prove that we—"

"Oh, but I have."

"Steve!"

Jacobs finally gets up. He feels his face tighten with anger and uncertainty. But looking down into McDaniel's calm, friendly eyes, for an instant he feels rather fatherly and protective. Suddenly he says something he doesn't expect to hear himself say: "I wouldn't be so cavalier if I were you, young man. You are in the middle of something very serious."

"Thank you for the free legal advice and for going on the record," says McDaniel. He raises his glass and smiles sincerely. "I'll make sure this conversation is published candidly."

Jacobs's demeanor transforms abruptly as he realizes the drinks, the country-club atmosphere of this Capitol Hill hangout, and McDaniel's relaxed manner and tone have all fooled him into saying more than he should have.

He is unsure what to say or do, or how to process what just happened. All he knows is suddenly he feels as if he is not in charge. He is a GS-15-level attorney in the nation's capital, and he has called the shots for so long he has forgotten that some people can still fight back. He is used to the authority of judges, of those up the chain of command, and people like McDaniel, outsiders who are under investigation, in his experience, have no power. The best they can do is negotiate from losing positions through their deal-making K Street attorneys. So why does he suddenly feel the power has shifted?

For just a flash of a moment, Sid thinks he might have to physically handle this government attorney, and it's not easy to defend oneself while seated in a cushy leather chair. But then, this attorney is a small, gray, flimsy little man who probably never even threw a punch in grade school. He just isn't used to being approached in public places by people he is in the process of abstractly destroying. He is used to the impersonal bureaucratic use of force, not to the street cop's first-person encounter. Steve hasn't even seen the inside of a courtroom since he was required to view legal proceedings in law school.

Jacobs seems to want to say something else, or perhaps he is wishing he could reverse the tape. Whatever is going on in his head, he is just standing there, looking down at Sid with the anxious look of a child peering out a front door into a moonless night.

Samson, who as an experienced journalist has engaged in a lot of in-person matches of wits, keeps his head, grabs Jacobs by the elbow, and leads him out.

Sid watches them go while sipping his sherry. Adam soon moves over and sits beside him in the chair Gary Samson had been seated in.

"How much did you get?"

"Everything between you and this government attorney," says Adam as he reaches under his chair and picks up a small microphone. "Quite a bit before you came in. I'll send you the audio file. What struck me was how blatant this Steve Jacobs was about it. Before you came in, he literally called it a *setup* when he referred to your involvement, but they clearly don't seem to know a lot. Those two aren't central players; they are useful idiots, just pawns in the big game."

Sid looks into the sherry in the clear, stemmed glass, "We have a lot more digging to do to get to the central players. Funny though, to see that attorney panic. He is used to being in control. The people he deals with, well, he handles them indirectly through their lawyers. Most cut deals, I suppose. If they don't, he'll find some procedural means to get their lawyers to make their clients give in to his power or connections. So he was out of his element. Anyway, sounds like I have my next column."

Adam shakes his head. "Back in Israel we would have just grabbed the people involved and brought them to a quiet place for an interrogation. I realize we can't do that here, but back there, when we couldn't grab them, we listened and watched. We waited and tracked them and noted who they were meeting—and, when possible, what they were saying. It took time, but sooner than you'd think, they'd show or tell us everything. Then we'd grab one, let him hear some of it, and offer him or her a deal. That works. But what you're doing, Sid, I don't quite get it. This could go either way. Most of the media is certainly not going to be with you. These agencies here in this town, they hold all the cards. They can leak and spin and give off-the-record tell-alls to media members friendly to their politics. They can beat you in the legal arena, because they can withhold anything for national security reasons. And they can beat you in the public arena with that same control of information. Instead, if we go slow, we can gather information and then use it to quietly make them cut a deal—or to at least make them back off."

Sid nods slowly. "Yes, that would be a smart way to play this. And you are right, I am playing fast and loose, all right. But they'll catch up, or on, sooner than later, so I need a lot of information fast. In the position I am in now, I can't get what I need by playing it slow and cool—well, I can't do that legally, anyway. They can get some FISA judge to rubber-stamp a wiretap or warrant, as they already have. Whereas I can't legally wiretap them."

"That's true," says Adam. "I wouldn't be any part of that, anyway."

"There is a lot here that baffles me." Sid eases back into the cushy chair and keeps his expression neutral. In this hip Washington watering hole, anyone could be watching or listening. "Those two don't want this document to come out, even though Samson was paid to assemble the opposition research. I suppose that can be explained by money and politics. The administration, via their Department of Justice, which oversees the FBI, is protecting itself. But that doesn't explain why I was brought into this."

"Do you want to back out, try to strike a deal?" asks Adam with hope in his eyes.

"Not yet. To win, I need to know what this is about—I don't necessarily have to use that information, but I do need to hold the cards. As it stands, if they leak and control the narrative at their pace, not mine, they can destroy me, as they know much more than I do. The politicians I need will only help me if there is some media on my side. So I need to knock this team, or whatever they are, fast and hard and repeatedly. I need them to flail out, to make mistakes, to make dumb moves because, in their bureaucracy, they don't have the time or the sense to do anything else."

Adam leans forward and rubs his palms on his bald head. "So you really don't know shit either."

"I know *they* are full of shit. I know they know it. I don't know a lot. But I do know they made a big mistake involving me in this."

"Watch me for tails," says Sid into his phone's headset as he walks down a sidewalk, in and out of the light from the streetlights.

"Given what I am hearing," says Jorge from the Bentley parked up with street, "the FBI will have a team on you soon."

"Is the shadow team you brought in set up?"

"Yes, they are spread out watching the players we've identified thus far."

"Good," says Sid. "I need to go pay a social call before my first column breaks later tonight."

It is a dark, star-filled night now, and he is walking into that ever-dangerous urban landscape, the parking garage. He sees people moving among autos parked between cement pillars and almost jumps when four-way lights flash as someone unlocks a Mini Cooper. He laughs out loud at himself then. He is hoping going fast will protect him, but knows he can't outrun this thing.

As is his habit, he runs a radio frequency detector over the bike. *Nothing yet.* He is actually disappointed they aren't yet trying to follow his motorcycle. He knows they'll begin that soon, but it worries him that it is taking them so long. They tossed his office and cabin. Tracking devices on his vehicles should have happened at the same time. But that's bureaucratic inefficiency for you. The New York FBI office is likely communicating with the D.C. team. Or maybe they're being careful about involving too many agents in this growing mess, so the local agents had to travel.

He sits on the motorcycle's black seat and turns on a phone. He dials Carole, chief of staff for Senator Haskins.

"Hi, it's Sid."

"Who?"

"Sid McDaniel. We met in Senator Haskins Capitol Building office."

"Oh."

"Time to get a drink?"

"Well," says Carole with her voice searching for a way to say yes without seeming too easy.

"How about Morton's, on the balcony? I'm hungry. You're from Iowa, you must like steak."

"Well, okay."

A quick ride under streetlights in the capital leads him to another underground parking garage. He leaves the bike and tells his team where it is. It is then a short walk and an escalator ride up in a glass building filled with closed shops, to Morton's. He is given a seat on the balcony at a corner table, with a view of the streets glowing with white streetlights and red taillights.

She is in a dress. It is blue and it doesn't cling. It is loose and moves with her slender legs. She has a yellow shawl for the spring evening chill on the balcony, and it is wrapped under her smile and feline eyes. He enjoys watching her walk, as if on her toes, between tables filled with groups of men smoking cigars and eating heavy food. He stands when she gets close and pulls out a metal chair for her.

He pushes her chair in and catches her perfume as he leans down.

"That's a lovely scent. What is it?"

"The perfume? Oh, just Maison Francis."

He has the sleeves on his white dress shirt rolled up just above his wrists. He has been sipping a whiskey neat and working out his next column on a laptop he closed when she entered.

"You've been working?"

"You have no idea."

"I hope I am not part of your work."

"You, no. I don't even know how men work around you."

She smiles and pushes aside her straight blonde, corn-belt hair.

"How often do you go home?" he asks.

"Christmas. And for a few weeks in the summer. We go on recess then, and summer air is so clean out in the country. Here, in The Swamp, it is so sultry and humid. But in Iowa the pool is cool in the day, and in the evening the wind filters through the corn and brings this sweet smell," says Carole.

"You're a poet."

"Now you're teasing me."

"No. No I am not. I could listen to you all night. I believe I will, if you'll let me," says Sid, holding her blue, blue eyes.

She almost blushes and he likes that.

"Where'd you go to school?"

"Iowa State and then Stanford."

"Must have been awful."

She laughs, and it is a lovely laugh. She doesn't even lose eye contact with him when she laughs. He likes that too.

"Where'd you go?" she asks and manages to make it sound flirtatious.

"MIT, but it didn't stick," he says.

"Oh, you're one of those."

"Those?"

"The creative types who are stifled by boundaries, bored with out-of-date books and minds that are behind the times."

The evening goes from steaks to a bottle of wine and then a walk along the gray sidewalks under the white streetlights of a city that can feel so much like a small town.

She never expected to take him home. She doesn't do that. But it comes so naturally. He doesn't ask to come in or even suggest she should invite him up to her second-floor flat. He just blows in with her on conversation that never stops, never has an awkward pause.

In the morning, after he is so gentle with her, she looks him in the eyes and asks, "Okay, what is it you want?"

"Just let me know," he says.

"What?"

"You'll know *what* when you hear it. Now tell me, please tell me you want to go out for breakfast," he says, looking into her eyes.

CHAPTER 7

It's mid-morning on Wednesday, and the walk to the parking garage where Sid left his motorcycle is exquisite. Cherry blossoms are in bloom along the river, and tulips are up in flower boxes on streets now busy with people hurrying about their lives. A few are jogging in the cool shadows of the late morning, but most are in suits or what passes for office casual these days.

He finally lets the pleasant dream that was the last twelve hours flit away and switches on a phone. As he knew they would, messages jolt him back into the uncomfortable reality of trying to prove he is not a spy by behaving like a spy.

"Your article is going viral," says a voicemail from Mack, the opinion editor. "We need to talk. I just got a call from the fucking Department of Justice. They threatened me with national security consequences if we publish any part of what everyone is calling the 'Dirty Document.' I don't like being threatened, but we'd better be careful here. They actually sound scared, and their fear scares the shit out of me."

Sid suppresses the urge to call Mack right back and clicks on the next message. "Be careful, Sid—seeing weird movement now among the players. Code red at your bike," says Jorge.

Sid steps close to a building to think for a moment before calling him back.

"Code red?"

"Yes. Red. There are two. A large one and a small one. They have a van. Be careful. Everything is ready."

"Okay." He hangs up and begins walking toward the parking garage on F Street again. His heart rate is up, and he takes deep breaths to bring it under control while he focuses on what must be done. When going into battle, the best plans are soon blown away, and so become nothing more than a direction to fight toward. He'll have to improvise now. He hopes he hasn't misjudged the lethality of this scene. He keeps walking toward it.

As he does, he continues going through the voicemails and listens to messages from TV and radio producers—dozens of them, forwarded from his overseas messaging service. Everyone wants him to come on and talk about his column, and to explain its insinuations and the direct quotes he has made public—quotes with audio links attached to them, so everyone can also hear Special Agent Baker, Gary Sampson, and DOJ attorney Steve Jacobs delivering their lines in their clear or arrogant tones.

He considers going on these shows and actually pictures himself giving the soundbites required for cable news. How could he ever sum this up in an entertaining way that doesn't sound all Deep State conspiratorial? If he does go on any of the shows, he'll have to calmly play the befuddled good man caught up in something he doesn't quite understand. There is a lot of truth in that. Just a week before, he was shocked to learn his name had been added as "Source E" to this illicit dossier, which was provided to the FBI. It was soon leaked to friendly members of Congress who are known to leak. But now the Department of Justice wants to kill the "Dirty Document" so badly they just threatened the opinion editor of the *New York Herald*.

This document could be viewed as a direct threat to the establishment, and thus to the Deep State; at least that is the most plausible reason for this strange ticking time bomb of circumstances. But still, a lot doesn't add up.

Yes, he'll need to be careful about how much he says, as he doesn't know enough yet to meander. If he did that, he could end up in trouble. He believes in Ernest Hemingway's Theory of Omission, which is that you can omit anything, and the omission will strengthen the point—if, that is, you really do know a lot more. If you don't, that'll come through, and you'll be seen as a faker, the peddler of a thin ideology in place of real knowledge or understanding.

So, if he does the media interviews, he'll simply end by saying Congress needs to hold public hearings to bring all of this into public light. He'll even say he can provide the names of the officials they need to have testify. That's all true, and it'll get these Deep State players moving.

Still, though he wants to continue to play a bold game, he doesn't want to play a foolhardy one, and this does feel crazy.

He takes a deep breath. He'll need to think about the public pressure this would create, and more about what he should say. Deep down he doesn't want to do the TV interviews, because he doesn't want to be a known face—at least not any more than he already is. Still, his gut is telling him he'd better do them now, before he is grabbed, before he is disappeared, or handed a gag order.

He turns off the phone. He thinks about this chess match with the government. He needs a little time to plan his next move. He needs to stay on the attack, of course, because he hasn't put them in check yet. He has simply moved out a few pieces to take an aggressive posture. Should he wait for a countermove? He isn't sure.

He finally decides that a morning ride in the warm spring air—maybe down to the George Washington Parkway to Mount Vernon, then back up past all of those parks and by the water—will do him good. But he first must deal with this "Code Red" waiting near his bike.

Sid steps into the dim light of the underground parking garage. An attendant watching him—too closely. There is a weird vibe from the man. He walks slowly down a ramp and turns right, past some blue pillars. He stops to put in a Bluetooth, but a man steps out from behind a van. The man is big and in a black flannel suit, and has the look of someone who has been waiting for him. His eyes slap Sid into fight-or-flight mode.

Sid clicks a button at the back of his belt to start the pinhole camera hiding in the white pocket square with red dots in his breast pocket.

The big man stops, but he doesn't stop his gray-eyed glare.

Sid pivots, instinctively feeling the urge to launch himself away, toward the ramp up to the street. But he finds two men behind him. They have been following him, and he should have noticed. They are in jogging shorts and t-shirts that bulge near their waists. Their new white sneakers squeak on the cement floor.

Another man, this one small and in a trim gray suit, steps out from behind a parked car. His eyes are as inquisitive as a rat's.

"We just want to talk," he says. He is maybe five foot four and older, with a Russian accent and the smooth, white complexion of a man from a northern city in the Russian Federation. He is smoking a cigarette and looks relaxed, in control, as his eyes search Sid's face. He has the skinny, drawn face of a man who has had to use his brains to move up.

Sid puts his hands on his hips and nods. "Okay, what do you want?"

"Not here," says the Russian, pointing his cigarette at a plain blue van parked between two compact cars.

"I am not going in there," says Sid with a tone that lets them know there will be a fight, a scene.

The Russian smiles.

The men in jogging outfits behind Sid move closer. The one in front of him, in the black suit—a man built well enough to wrestle professionally—is now just five steps away.

"We have information for you," says the Russian with the cigarette. "We have a shared interest and can help you. We know the players you're up against in your own government."

Sid nods again and lets out a long breath. "You must like the chaos of this—and, especially, what's to come."

The Russian smiles a yellow-tooth smile. "Our information is good."

"I am sure it is as good as the hacked DNC emails you passed to Wikileaks."

The Russian draws a long puff, flaring the cigarette. "Even the DNC didn't dispute the authenticity of those. Not that I am taking credit for that data, but only a buffoon uses the password 'password.'"

Sid doesn't like being anywhere near these Russians. He'll be tainted if news of this clandestine meeting comes out in the wrong way. The bad actors he is trying to shake out of the government would paint him with guilt by association, and the media would use it to discredit him. He wonders if that's precisely what these Russians want, but he doesn't have time now to dwell on the thought.

With his left hand, the Russian takes something out of an inside breast pocket of his suit. It looks to be a little black flash drive. He places it on his left palm and holds it out for Sid to see as he begins to walk forward. The garage is suddenly so quiet he can hear the Russian's Oxfords on the gray cement.

Sid then hears the man on his right move. This man raises a hand. *A gun?* No, he realizes; the guy is shooting video.

Blackmail.

Sid looks back into the eyes of the Russian approaching him with the thumb drive in his outstretched hand. Sid drops his hands to his sides and brings his right foot a shoulder's width behind his left. He tries not to change his expression as he does this. He simply maintains eye contact with the man approaching him. He feels more than sees the others step closer.

When the Russian with the cigarette is nearly an arm's length distant, Sid turns on his left foot and pivots his hips. With the speed of a boxer's jab, his right knee comes up and his right leg spins around from behind, smashing out and straight into the Russian's chest. The blow knocks the small man off his feet backwards into a parked car. His cigarette flies somewhere over the car, and the thumb drive slides under the car, whose horn starts to scream, echoing in the underground garage. The Russian tumbles to the floor, holding his chest and groaning.

The other three Russians rush Sid. The two closest have phones out, recording, which makes them clumsy and slow. Sid spins low with a sweep kick and knocks the one on his left into the other. Both fall on top of each other. One of their phones cracks against the cement floor.

Sid doesn't pause. He uses the momentum of the sweep kick to pop up and accelerate toward the ramp out to the street. The guy in the dark suit is just behind him. The car's alarm keeps blaring, and its headlights and four-ways flash in the fluorescent light of the underground garage. He hears the others cursing in Russian.

Sid hears the big Russian's feet pounding and his lungs already gasping, and he has no trouble outpacing the thug as he races up the ramp and out onto the bright sidewalk. He turns left and keeps running for a hundred feet. Then he pauses to look back.

The big Russian has thought better of pursuing Sid on the sunny sidewalks of downtown Washington. He stops, glances at people staring at him, clenches his big fists, and bends over to breathe for a few seconds. Then he turns around and disappears back into the garage.

Sid continues on and turns left at a corner. He goes another few hundred feet, then stops and leans against a wall of a building in the shade of a small tree.

"Jorge," he says, a phone to his ear while he grabs a few deep breaths.

"Yes, I'll let you know when it's clear. Adam is closer than I am," whispers Jorge.

Sid begins to catch his breath. Five minutes later Adam calls and says in terse whispers, "There is another team. They're just watching. We have some photos of them. The Russians piled into the van they wanted you to get into and are now leaving. Wait until you hear what they said after you got out of there. We stashed a lot of mics, so the audio is good enough for a Hollywood production."

Sid laughs. To his right, he sees the blue van going fast up F Street, away from the White House. The windows are down; the big Russian in the dark suit is driving, and the little man Sid kicked is yelling at him from the passenger seat while pointing a lighted cigarette at him, like it's a gun. The van changes lanes to pass a sedan, then speeds through a yellow light.

"It's like a Monty Python skit," says Sid as he watches them go.

He walks back to the corner of the building and peeks around to see the entrance of the underground garage.

"I didn't expect you to kick him," says Jorge in Sid's ear, still whispering.

"Why not? You helped me perfect that move."

"Right, but wow—you just spin-kicked a Russian agent. A little one, but KGB nonetheless. I was in the Green Berets ten years and never got to do that."

"It was the only thing I could think to do," says Sid. "I couldn't risk being blackmailed by them, because they'd have video of me taking a thumb drive from them in a damned parking garage. Who and where is the other team?"

"They're leaving now," says Adam. "FBI, likely. Feds for sure."

A black SUV with tinted windows comes out of the parking garage, followed by a sports car, a black Maserati. The two vehicles turn right, go to a light, then both turn left without using their turn signals.

"All clear," says Adam.

Sid steps out onto the sidewalk beneath small leafy trees, walks to the entrance of the underground garage, and goes down the ramp. Halfway down he stops to look at the garage's attendant. The man is young with dark, greasy hair. His countenance is wrapped in fear and confusion—like a young dog that knows it was bad and now just doesn't want to be punished for going on the floor.

"How much did the Russians pay you?"

The attendant goes into his little glass booth, sits, and pretends to do paperwork.

Sid continues down into the ramp, turns right, and stops at his motorcycle, where Adam is waiting for him.

"We swept it," says Adam, continuing to sweep for signals around the bike. "Just one little tracking device. It's an FBI tool.

Look." He holds out the little device. "You can tell by the mold. The NSA actually has a patent on this part here," he says, pointing to circuitry. "A secret one, of course. I only know because they enforced this patent a few years ago, when an Israeli contractor built something similar and tried to take it out commercially. Funny that you only learn about their patents when or if they enforce them."

"Put it back on the bike," says Sid. "I'll let them tag along until I find a use for them."

Adam nods and sticks the device back under the seat, which juts out from the bike's frame over the rear tire.

Sid asks, "That was Agent Baker in the Maserati wasn't it?"

"Sure was." Jorge steps out from between two cars. He is in a black hoodie and jeans, and his eyes are tired, but his voice is full of life. "She nearly had me. She parked just two cars away from me. She was observing."

"How about the others?"

"They were in a black four-door SUV," says Adam. "Could've spotted that vehicle at a glance—a special model with heavily tinted windows. But they did get a good position—over there at the end, where they could see everything from a good distance. We were just here much earlier."

"Photos of them?"

"We got photos and video of two of them. And that Agent Baker, of course," says Adam. "Our supplementary team has the street. I don't know what they have yet. Certainly license plates and all that."

"I didn't see them out there," says Sid.

"Good to hear that a Navy SEAL can enter a scene without making it all about himself," says Jorge. He then rolls his eyes, shakes his head, and starts laughing as he says, "I have John, ah, the former SEAL, on another feed. He just told me to stick a green beret in my ass and then pull it back out and check the color."

"Ask him," says Sid, "how you can tell when a Navy SEAL is in the room."

"He heard you, and I'm not going to repeat what he is saying."

"Good. He knows the punchline: 'They're going to tell you,'" says Sid. "By the way, when did the feds get here?"

"An hour ago," says Adam.

"Think they were staking out my bike, or did they have some advanced intel on the Russians?"

"The Russians," says Adam. "The timing was too coincidental, and they were so calm about it. They weren't surprised. Also, the way they set up—classic watch and see. Without the Russians, there wouldn't have been much to see."

"Makes sense that they'd have this Russian team under surveillance," says Jorge. "I did enough of that in Syria."

"But what was it the Russians wanted to get out of this?" asks Adam.

"Us, possibly," says Sid. "We've been a pest to them and their hacks of major U.S. corporations for years. Our investigations have even gotten a few of them thrown out of the country. If this leaks, though, my reputation, and therefore my company, will be done."

"That adds up. Now what?" asks Jorge.

"First," says Sid with a sigh as his mind adjusts, "we need to consider our phones compromised. Follow protocol to change again."

Jorge and Adam nod. This annoyance is so routine it's no longer something they even complain about. They buy phones a bundle at a time; link them to encrypted cloud accounts cloaked behind foreign VPNs, to access contacts and more; and then wipe and toss the phones regularly. Their biggest worries are state-sponsored corporate spies from China and, to a lesser extent, from Russia, but there are many private hacker groups and governments they need to keep out of their communications, as well.

"You guys look tired," says Sid, looking from one to the other in the dim light of the garage.

"Yeah, we were on stakeout all night, as you were...well, working your pretty contact," says Jorge.

"Ah, the jealousy of a married man. Get some sleep," says Sid, "but do let me know what you have. I need to decide what to go public with. I'll clear my head by taking the FBI for a ride first."

"Park your bike out front of the townhome when you get there," says Adam, as Sid unplugs his motorcycle from a charging station. "We've set up a surveillance perimeter, and that bike's suite of cameras will help."

"We sure loaded this motorcycle."

Adam is laughing, "Yes, it's a moving television studio."

"Isn't it time to move to another house?" asks Sid. He is used to calling the shots, but when it comes to physical security, he defers to Jorge and Adam's expertise.

Jorge looks at Adam, and they both look at Sid.

"One day out on a mission in Afghanistan, we ran into an ambush," says Jorge slowly and seriously. "We had two A-Teams—twenty-four men—and forty ANA soldiers as we went deep into the Taliban's backyard. As it got dark, we took our Humvees out onto a salt flat. It was pancake flat for a mile around. We didn't want to hide, as there was no hiding. It is their terrain. We needed to see them coming. We owned the night, and we knew it, and they knew it. Same here. There is a time to hide in a population, but this isn't it. We have the perimeter, and the inside of that townhome is all set up for them. If they come, we'll expose them and everything they say and do."

"Okay," says Sid, "this certainly isn't a gunfight—or it better not be. It's a fight we win with the First Amendment."

Adam says, "I agree. This is how I did it at the embassies. We set traps and waited where we could see them coming."

All three look at each other for a quiet moment. None of them like this. But they decided together to take this fight to the enemy, whoever they turn out to be. They all silently nod and step back.

Sid pushes on his black motorcycle helmet, pulls the bike back, and lets it take him up the ramp and out into the sun and traffic.

CHAPTER

8

Sid spends an hour driving in light traffic down to Mount Vernon and then back up the George Washington Memorial Parkway under the trees and sun, letting the buildings and parks blur. He believes he has his thoughts together when his Bluetooth beeps in his ear.

"We fucked up!"

"What's that, Adam?"

"We were so focused on trying to find out who involved you in this and why, that we missed what this is all about."

Adam pauses, and it's a long pause.

"You have me hanging on your every word." Sid sits, barely moving, behind a series of red taillights on the Fourteenth Street Bridge going into Washington.

"We thought Global Positions just dredged up some uncomfortable stuff on the president, and that the Deep State or the establishment or whatever was simply moving to protect him."

"Well, aren't they?"

"Yes, of course, as is much of the media," says Adam, "but there is something much bigger."

Adam over-emphasizes the word "bigger" and stops.

"Again, I am hanging on your every word."

Sid can almost see Adam holding the phone with his left hand as he habitually rubs the top of his shaved head with his right hand, and as his eyes sink back into his ever-deep worrisome pool of thoughts.

Adam finally says, "Well, this is still coming into focus, but I started following leads in the 'Dirty Document' and its footnotes, which led me to this president's son's business partners in Ukraine, Russia, and China. After a little digging, I found that some of them got screwed over. They didn't get paid. They didn't get their cut. The president's son, Buck, took the money and blew it—literally."

"So?"

"So, these are informants who've worked for Western governments many times and they're mad. If they got their cut, they'd never say a word, but they didn't. Their bitching has made waves in the intel community. A lot of FBI and CIA agents had to run around to settle down these sources with money. It's like having to run around behind a no-good relative who is writing bad checks. The creditors are angry and will call the cops, so you have to make the debts good.

"This 'Dirty Document,'" Adam goes on, "is filthy with connections like this. It leads to a web of informants, often on corporate boards, who have been paid to give dirt, as those companies are all basically state run. And the U.S. intel community has its paws all over this. They have used these same informants and others like them to check on the president, on the president before him, and on others. This FBI program goes way back. I have contacts telling me I'd better stop pulling at this thread. They're scared because it could expose spying that U.S. intelligence agencies have been doing on presidential campaigns for at least the last four administrations—maybe all the way back to J. Edgar Hoover's FBI, for all I know. When Gary Samson's contractors began digging away at the president's son's business dealings, they began to unravel this."

"How do you know this?" Sid asks.

"Some of the contractors Global Positions used are former intelligence for the United Kingdom's SIS, France's DGSI, Israel's Mossad—and many government officials in Ukraine and elsewhere have also been involved. A retired contractor Samson hired gave me a lot, as I've known him for years. Look, the intel community is a small field at the top. Many of these people know each other."

"How could this document unearth all that?"

"Sid, wake up!" screams Adam, a man who rarely even breaks a sweat when he works out. "Because of the president's stupid, greedy, crack-addicted son Buck, that's how. He has unwittingly exposed a program long run by the FBI's Counterespionage Section, which is now headed by Neil Kuntz. They vet presidents—partly legally, as they are partly responsible for doing background checks on candidates to determine what they can and can't tell them—but this keeps going even when an elected official is in office. This gives the Deep State the information, and that information is power. They can influence the outcomes of campaigns with leaks and nudges. They can use the information, whether it is good or not, to pressure or guide sitting presidents. They usually get their way with who gets to be president, but not always. When they don't, they do other setups. Perjury traps, for one—some of that went public with the last administration. More often they just quietly pressure presidents during Oval Office meetings by letting them know what they have on them and their families. In this way, these U.S. intel lifers are pulling the levers of our so-called democratic republic."

Adam pauses a moment. When he speaks again, his voice is low.

"This is too hot, Sid. We need to find a way out, and fast. These people will kill us."

While Adam speaks, Sid has been navigating Washington's streets to Columbus Circle, finding street parking just east of Union Station on Third Street NE, between F and E Streets.

"Adam, this is insane. Are you sure?"

"This is a little-known-or-talked-about, high-level, and very-top-secret program, but yes, it is real. It's a program they all simply refer to as 'Operation Vet the President.' First, they infiltrate campaigns and investigate candidates, and then after the elections, this operation continues to spy on presidents and their staffs. When you think about it, you'll find it makes sense for the intelligence agencies to do much of this. They need to know if these people have any issues or vulnerabilities to being blackmailed by foreign governments or entities. That's the standard security-clearance part that gives this whole thing cover. But they take it several big steps further by spying with warrantless taps, by using paid informants, and, later, by using the info to empower themselves and to protect their power. It's not hard to see how this sort of secret power can corrupt. Look, obviously I can't use names, even though we're using an encrypted app to talk. But yes, dammit, yes, I was just told by someone in the know that I'd be smart to drop this thing fast, and then to let the relevant powers know in no uncertain terms that we are walking away."

Sid gets off the motorcycle and stretches his back, but keeps the black motorcycle helmet on as he speaks into the Bluetooth. "How could we even do that? No, I hear you, but to protect ourselves we need something that they know would come out if they kill us. And they're not just going to take our word for it."

"Sid, a lot of pieces are coming together. Remember those two special agents who thought you were a stuck-up, rich shit as they looked over your suits in your Uptown place?"

"Sure."

"They are Special Agents Jake Halperin and Paul Loring."

"So?"

"Their fathers are politicians. Jake's father is Congressman Mike Halperin, a Democrat representing a district in Illinois. Paul's father is merely a state senator in Michigan."

"What are you getting at?"

"They've both interned and have held other roles in various politician's campaigns," says Adam. "Halperin even worked inside the current president's campaign as an IT specialist. He has an undergrad computer-science degree from Johns Hopkins. Before this president was in office, and for a while after the election, Halperin had access to all of the president's communications. Then, just before the president was sworn into office, Halperin wound up at the FBI Academy at Quantico. Clearly, he has been a useful part of this program for years."

Sid is quiet. He doesn't know what to say, but that makes sense. So many treat IT professionals as if they are plumbers. If you have a computer problem, you just call them in and let them rove around your system. When they come from a trusted background, such as the son of a congressman, then they are trusted implicitly by an older generation—a generation that doesn't know such a person can see and copy every email, text, and search. Halperin would have been an obvious recruit or a good plant for such an FBI program.

Still, Sid doesn't have time for this. Exasperated, he says, "But dammit, this still doesn't explain who involved us in this—and why. We need more. We need to understand this so we can make a deal or something. Right now, what can I bargain with? Just telling them that we really, really will leave them alone isn't bargaining power; that just would be telling them we are indeed a threat they have to take seriously."

"Yeah, I suppose there is nowhere in the world to hide from this," says Adam as his voice trails off like a dying summer breeze.

"Keep digging, Adam, but be careful. We don't want to alert the FBI that we're poking around in all that."

"Okay, Sid."

"I am going on TV. They want me to talk about my column."

"Don't do it." Adam's voice is suddenly strong again.

"Relax. I won't talk about this. I just want to put some pressure on these people, whoever they are, so they'll move so fast they'll make mistakes."

"Sid, you need to at least try to strike a deal with the government. Going on a cable news channel isn't the way to do that. That'll just freak them out. You need to see if you can make this go away before they decide to make *you* go away. Then you can go back to the good life—you know, working undercover for Fortune 500s that have been hacked or that have moles committing corporate espionage, and slipping away now and then to Spain or southern Africa or whatever."

Sid is nodding to himself, seeing those places from memories, and wishing he was back at his cabin beneath the quiet green trees. He knows it is good advice, if it'll work. He doesn't think it would, not without something big to bargain with. Also, he doesn't know why the notion of bargaining is like bad milk in his mouth.

"Objection noted. Stay in touch."

Sid hangs up, takes off his helmet, and secures it to the bike. The major cable news studio he is going to is a short walk from Union Station and up in a glass building. He starts heading there.

As he walks west past the U.S. Securities and Exchange Commission to Columbus Circle, he shakes his head at all the stuff this government does in secret. Much of it is necessary, or at least explainable, but an uncomfortable amount is pure politics and mistrust of elected officials they don't control—and of the public.

The traffic is heavy on this Wednesday afternoon. He pauses at crosswalks with a waiting crowd, then strides across the busy streets in front of Union Station. The shadows cast by the newly green trees across from the Circle are long, and the air is warm and florid. Candy-colored tulips stand like lollipops along well-landscaped edges. Sid worries that he might be too calm in light of this new revelation. It is never good to be too relaxed when walking into a volatile situation. It is better to be a little on edge, to have a cat's awareness and reflexes, not the dog's careless, tongue-hanging grin.

Sid is also concerned that he is actually enjoying this hunt, this chess match, too much. This is a dangerous game to play. He is in the arena with Deep State thugs, and he worries he is having too much fun to think rationally. Even if he gets to the bottom of this, all he can really win is his freedom, which is what he'd get by cutting a deal, anyway. He wonders if he is indeed a closet idealist, as Bob Steward believes. After all, why else would he care if some Deep State goons play around with dangerous things, like who gets to be president?

If it's just the thrill of the hunt he is addicted to, then what does this say about his life? Is he really that bored? In many of his jobs, he has taken on the hacking teams of Chinese and Russian billionaires—people who are used to crushing any journalist, activist, or other idealist who gets in their way. Those challenges have hardly been dull. They are why he takes so many precautions. And these successful hunts have made him comfortably wealthy. So what is the point in taking these outrageous risks?

Is he just an adrenaline junkie? He hopes that's not it. Sure, he loves to climb and often goes solo up rock faces in the Gunks. He also has found that he enjoys fighting. He doesn't want to be known for this, and he certainly doesn't want to fight in some ring or octagon with people watching, but he does deeply enjoy very technical matches on the mats with skilled adversaries who want to submit him or knock him cold. Is that what this is about, the love of a good fight?

Another light changes, and he trots across an intersection.

The simple love of a good fight doesn't feel like the answer—maybe part of the answer, but not the basis of it. Could it be pride? He was angry that they dragged him into this by tweaking the metadata to make it look like he had a hand in gathering this alleged information about the president. But he has never been the vengeful type. He has always been able to walk away from unnecessary fights. He loves that other people's guilt, their criticism, and their harsh characterizations don't stick to him or goad him. He just walks away clean and feels untainted, knowing they are only projecting and acting defensively because of their own problems and shortcomings.

So, if it isn't idealism, adrenaline, the love of a good fight, or his hurt pride, then what is it?

He is in the building now. He shows his ID to security and is led into a small, windowless "green room." He recognizes the three pundits in the simple chairs along the walls and is happy they don't recognize him. He is surprised that they don't ask who he is—but then, he isn't.

These are high-profile pundits, and each has his own lane, and an unknown isn't even in the hierarchy. They aren't questioning much. They aren't nosy reporters. They are well-paid partisans, entrenched in their established ideology, invited there to deliver a safe establishment point of view. They are ready to counter, good-naturedly of course, the opposing point of view they know will be in the room with them. They, and their opponents, are happy and willing participants in the mainstream media narratives. They are comfortable with the idea there are only two sides to any discussion, just as there are only two political parties in America worth taking seriously.

Sid takes a seat, crosses his legs, ignores them right back, and falls back into thought.

Does he really want to take these people down because he finds them to be unpalatable bad actors? Is he really so self-righteous? He is not a police officer. He is more like a contract killer—he takes out bad actors. No, he has never been an idealist, not completely. He deals in facts, in code, in numbers, and then, yes, in the often unfathomable hearts of men.

But then, many women have accused him of being self-righteous. He has always thought this to be a shallow misunderstanding; he thinks they come to this conclusion simply because he can't be fit into their suburban dreams. It's a fantasy where they capture an urban lion in New York City, tame him, then move the beast of the urban jungle to the sedate 'burbs, where they chain him comfortably to a mortgage, kids, and a golden retriever. And why not? It works with men often enough. So when it doesn't work with him, they need to find fault that's not in themselves.

Sid keeps slipping the tender trap, and they are out of his life before they've really gotten to know him. He only lets them in so deep before he becomes disappointed with something in them or in himself. He then politely cuts them loose. And he does do it politely. He genuinely helps them and has even helped a few meet someone they are much more compatible with. This is why he has decided that these women's opinions of him are simply the result of them running into a man with deep and well-founded convictions, who knows who he is and what he wants; and so they simply mistake these earned beliefs for self-righteousness.

Such is what he thinks. But he isn't really sure. He does know this is a belief system he'll have to challenge soon, because he can't really know if he is right until he finds a woman, a relationship, big enough and deep enough to upend this convenient view of himself.

He looks at the other three in the green room, buried in their phones, and is relieved that they do *not* want to talk politics with him.

He is much more interested in the foundation of the system, anyway. He thinks this is why he is into computer code. He is most interested in what makes things tick. As such, his philosophy is deeply rooted in Edmund Burke, David Hume, John Locke, and others who broke free, and both realized and built upon the idea of the autonomous individual. This clean, empowering, and humbling ideal of individual rights—the idea that the individual supersedes the state—is beautiful to him, as it was, in theory, to the Founders of America. So no, he isn't for one party or the other, but for a deeper ideal, for a system that is freeing, not controlling, in an age when the establishment in both parties wants control—when one, perhaps, just wants it more.

His meandering thoughts are interrupted when a producer steps into the green room and says, "Sid McDaniel."

He stands and the pundits in the room stop talking. He can tell they're wondering who Sid McDaniel is.

He is wearing his blue Brioni, this time with a blue-and-red striped tie. He is not carrying anything. He has silenced his two phones. He isn't thinking anymore about what he will say. He decided what needs to be said while on his drive to Mount Vernon.

He follows the producer through a door, down a hall, and into a small studio. There is a chair facing lights and cameras. The host of this afternoon show is in New York City. Sid will hear the host via an earpiece, but won't be able to see anyone—just bright lights and the glass lenses of cameras.

He finds the lights annoying, but what is really vexing is that he must remember the camera is watching him without blinking. He has to maintain the correct facial expressions even though he can't see the host, and even though he doesn't know if he is being shown at any particular time on television screens. The producer didn't even tell him how long the segment would be.

After a minute, he hears the host reading part of his opinion article. He assumes it's on the television screen for all to read.

"So we have Sid McDaniel, a computer forensics expert and opinion columnist, here to explain this alleged dossier on the president that has now gone public. We're not showing or even quoting from this so-called dossier—or, as some are calling it, the 'Dirty Document'—as none of its salacious details have been verified. But it's not hard to find on the internet. Some of it is seedy, allegedly personal stuff. Other parts insinuate payments with and to Russian and Chinese state-backed firms. So Mr. McDaniel, have you learned anything concerning the truth about this alleged information on the president of the United States?"

"Yes," says Sid before continuing slowly, hoping the calm pace will allow his words to sink in. "I learned last week, thanks to a journalist looking for verification, that I was somehow involved in this so-called 'Dirty Document.' I quickly got my team working on the data behind it. We traced it back to several IP addresses and then to several people. We are still investigating, but we have already proven through analysis of the metadata in this document that my name's inclusion was an attempt to give this document an air of authenticity."

"Wait a second," says the cable news host, "do you know who was behind this dossier on the president?"

"I do. An opposition-research firm called Global Positions was hired to put this dossier together. They, in turn, used independent contractors, many with former intelligence agency connections, to gather the material in this document. Those intel professionals then hired Russian and Chinese expats who now live in the U.S. and in Europe, to provide what amounts to gossip and innuendo, though there are a lot of audio and video attachments to this document. These appear to be edited, but it is not yet clear, at least to me, if any of this information can be trusted."

"So who hired Global Positions to produce this dossier in the first place?"

"Interestingly, it was initially funded by prominent members of the president's party. But then, after he had all but secured the nomination, it was funded by the other party. The document wasn't made public during the election, but U.S. intelligence agencies have had this file of opposition research for some time."

Sid pauses to wait for a response or question. He next wants to go deeper into this explosive story, telling his part in all of this. But instead the host says, "Hold on."

There is five seconds of dead air before the cable-news host says, "We have breaking news. The FBI has just raided a Russian-owned-and-run facility in Maryland. An official statement from the FBI says they are deporting various Russian spies who are associated with this dossier."

The host asks, "Sid McDaniel, as you are an expert in computer hacking and more, what is your reaction to this raid?"

"It sounds like they are talking about Pioneer Point," says Sid.

"Yes, that is what this official statement says. Do you know anything about this property?"

"Not about this raid or what's behind it, as it's news to me," says Sid, "but Pioneer Point is a well-known Russian-government-owned property. I've dealt with corporate espionage traced to that location many times. After researching it, I found that U.S. intelligence agencies are well aware of this property, and have been since the Russians bought it in 1972.They keep a close eye on it—just as the Russians no doubt do with properties our government owns in Moscow."

"So this has been going on for a long time?"

"Oh yes, Pioneer Point is a forty-five-acre estate on Maryland's Eastern Shore. It is treated by the Russians as state property, and therefore is protected by diplomatic immunity," says Sid. "As I said, a few of my investigations into hacked companies have dead-ended there. I reported this each time to the FBI. They acknowledged receipt of the data I shared, but that's all. I don't know why they are raiding it now."

"Hold on," says the host again, "we have to take a quick break."

The cable-news host's voice sounds a little rattled and this break is sudden. Sid is left sitting in a little room, looking into cameras and bright lights, not knowing what's going on.

A minute later he hears the host go to a Russian expert they use as a contributor. This expert is on a phone line. Sid listens to him and waits, but is never invited back into the conversation. His feed goes dead, and a moment later a producer pops into the room.

"Well, wait," says Sid, "I have news to break here."

"I am sorry," says the producer nervously. Her eyes are darting around. She doesn't want to make eye contact with Sid. "Maybe we can have you on again. I don't know. Right now, you have to go."

This producer's tone is rushed, even a little frightened. Sid walks close to her and tries to make eye contact. She steps back and looks away.

"What's going on," he asks, almost in a whisper.

"Please, just leave."

He steps even closer to her, personally close, looks her in the eyes, and says—still very calmly, as a person will when they really need help but no one is listening: "*Please*, tell me."

"Okay, look," she says as she steps back again and moves next to sound-reducing paneling on a wall. "There is video of you taking something from a Russian agent in a parking garage or something. It was just emailed to us. It's one of the Russians who was just deported. We can't have you in here."

Her voice is as rigid as breaking ice.

"Who sent this to you?"

"Off the record, a Department of Justice contact," she says and her face flushes, knowing she shouldn't have even said that much.

Sid thanks her and walks out of the glass building. They are now playing fast chess with him, and they have made a solid move, putting him into check. He also realizes he was too far ahead of the news for these producers to understand what he was getting at. He has been outmaneuvered in the big game of politics, leaks, backroom deals, and public exhibitions.

He'll need to move faster and smarter now.

CHAPTER 9

"I shouldn't even be talking to you," says Mack Davis instead of saying "hello" when he answers Sid's call.

"What are you talking about?" Sid is seated at a small table outside The Dubliner, an Irish-style pub and restaurant near Union Station. His back faces the restaurant's windows, a laptop is open in front of him, and he is sipping whiskey. The streetlights are just beginning to come on as the sunlight fades away.

"Don't you watch TV?"

"I was just on it." Sid says wearily.

"This is everywhere."

"I know. I need to place a column tonight. I'm sending it to you now," says Sid as he taps keys on his laptop.

"I can't do that!" shouts Mack. "Look, there is video of you taking some illegally hacked info from a Russian agent this morning. There is video all over the news. Some are even saying you're with the *New York Herald*. Damn it! They say the Russians were giving you Top Secret information on U.S. intelligence agencies."

"It's not true," Sid says simply.

"But there is video!"

"Yes, and I have video of the entire incident. I'll send you the unedited copy. It'll show they are lying."

"You have something to back up what you're telling me?"

"I have everything. I want to release this in conjunction with my next column. But you have to be strong, Mack. The FBI is moving now. They are sure to attempt to stop you from publishing what I send."

"How would they know?"

"Damn it, Mack, tapping your phone is standard in this kind of investigation."

"Shit."

"Look, Mack, they're going to arrest me. Soon, I think. I can't say more on this line, but you have to keep an open communication with my team."

"Shit," says Mack again before he hangs up.

Jorge is there with a Guinness in his left hand and a touch of white foam on his upper lip. He sits down in front of Sid, facing the restaurant, and places the dark beer on a coaster between them. All around them are crowded tables humming with the conversation of people beginning to let loose after a day at the office. Inside, the evening crowd is at the bar. The air is cool, but not cold, and faint floral smells are mixed with the exhaust blowing in from all the autos along Massachusetts Avenue.

Jorge settles back into a cold metal chair, looking tired. The creases on his face seem deeper, and Sid notices the gray on the temples of his buzzed-short hair.

"We still have those photos of Mack, right?" asks Sid as he hits "Send" and closes the laptop.

"With those, *ah*, professional women? Sure. His feet getting cold?"

"Frightened as a six-year-old alone in a dark tent."

"Oh, boy." Jorge rocks forward, then back into his chair and brings his arms up over his head to stretch his shoulders and back.

"And they're going to arrest me."

Jorge lowers his arms. "How do you know?"

"It's the only play they have, given the silly move they just made."

Jorge's eyebrows go up, and his brown eyes are now very alert.

"They've gone public with a video of the Russians who waited for me in that parking garage," Sid continues. "Only theirs is a clip edited to make it look like I took that flash drive."

"What?"

"Now we need to go public with our video. Don't edit what you release. Just let our proxies put the raw footage everywhere. And send a copy to Mack, pronto."

"Okay."

Jorge takes a long sip of his Guinness. He puts the glass down slowly on the coaster and stares at the draught for a moment. When he looks up, he sees Sid slumped back into his chair with an expression that looks like resolved indifference.

Then Sid slides his laptop into a soft leather case and hands it to him, before saying, "Now I need you to fade into the background and make sure the team gets full records of whatever they do to me here. I am switching on my phones and other devices and linking the audio to our databases in the cloud. Maybe we'll get lucky."

Jorge looks into Sid's eyes and places his right hand on the man's shoulder. "Don't worry, Sid. We'll be out here making the moves we've already discussed. Whatever happens, we'll be here."

Sid nods, but for the first time, Jorge is worried. He has reason to be. Sid has this crumpled look, as if he has turned fatalistic all of a sudden. Jorge has seen this look before—on wounded men who are in the process of giving up. They sink then, and soon they are so difficult to bring back around to life, to hope. They are like athletes who give up and just go through the motions to a loss.

He decides not to tell Sid what he sees. Saying it would make it real, and he hopes Sid is just mentally resting, maybe shifting gears, before being arrested. Soldiers do that before battle. Fighters do that before they enter the ring.

Jorge's eyes move from Sid to the people in the crowded restaurant, and then back to Sid. He still loves being on a mission, but in the Special Forces, they'd make a plan as an A-Team, practice it for maybe weeks, and then execute it. There was always improvising in the throes of the action, but not like this. This has too many moving parts. Too many uncertainties. It's a battle of moves and countermoves with his own government.

He stands and takes the laptop with him as he slips into the after-work crowd washing out onto the sidewalk along F Street NW.

A few minutes later, Sid spots a white cable news van with big red letters on its side pulling off Massachusetts Avenue onto F Street in front of the restaurant. He sighs and sips his Jameson, watching as the news crew gets out, then sets up cameras in the evening light. He knows this is a scene in which he is supposed to play the bad guy, but he doesn't feel like a bad guy, and he certainly doesn't want to play one on national TV.

He recognizes a Washington newspaper reporter a moment later. He notices others gathering outside with notepads in their hands and cameras ready. They are easy to spot, staring at the restaurant and talking to each other on the sidewalk. He looks for the FBI agents and spots two. They are stiff and serious, and one young agent keeps touching the concealed gun in his shoulder holster, as if he needs to assure himself it is still there.

Sid slowly picks up his little glass and takes a last sip, feeling the warmth of the whiskey sliding down his throat. Then he rises, steps between the small metal tables filled with people, beers, and fish-and-chips platters, and walks out to the sidewalk.

It's six o'clock now, and the evening light is fading from reds to blues. Some men in dark, off-the-rack suits start to follow him. One is speaking urgently into his suit jacket.

Sid crosses F Street and stops in front of the TV cameras. He stands there trying to make eye contact with them, but they think he is just a curious onlooker. They don't know him by sight. He finds this to be a relief. Finally he just says, loudly, to the person who looks to be the on-camera personality, "Hi, I'm Sid McDaniel. I believe you are here to capture me being perp-walked. How about an interview first?"

The reporter is befuddled. She turns and looks at her camera crew, but they just shrug. A print reporter steps forward. "I'd love an interview."

"Good," Sid says loudly, like an actor projecting his voice on a stage. "I'll talk to all of you. This is now a press conference. My name is Sid McDaniel. I own and run a computer-forensics firm based in New York City. This morning a Russian agent tried to give me a flash drive. I don't know what was on it. I kicked the Russian in the chest. He fell backward into a parked car. I had to outrun the other Russians. I have video of this entire scene. My team is now making it public. It'll show that whoever released the footage that brought you all here edited their version to push a lie. The truth is I didn't get anything, and I never have. The truth is FBI agents picked up that flash drive. I have video of that too."

A gathering crowd is listening, confused, but intrigued. The reporters are scribbling notes and cameras are running.

"I have also traced this so-called dossier—the 'Dirty Document,' as some are calling it. Both major political parties, at different times, funded it. What's really interesting—"

He is grabbed from behind and thrown face-down on the pavement. Handcuffs are clamped tight to his wrists, held behind his back, a knee is hard on his spine, and rough hands search him and take his phones, keys, and other items. One of these hands takes his little pocketknife, a keepsake he was given by a Scout Master when he was a boy.

He is then yanked up to his feet and held there for a moment for the cameras to see.

He tastes blood on his lip, but feels a surge of defiance as they pose him, hands cuffed behind his back. He feels like he is still playing the good guy in what has become an action film, so he shouts: "You'll all have the unedited video soon. I hope you'll have the guts to air it."

He is pulled away by strong grips on his arms. Spectators are pushed aside along the street, and he is propelled by a hand on his neck and others on his back into a waiting black Suburban.

These FBI agents and police officers are letting Sid know, with grunts and rough treatment, that they clearly don't like playing the bad guys.

He is positioned in the center of a bench seat behind the driver with his hands still cuffed behind his back. Young special agents in dark suits are jammed in on both sides of him, their shoulders touching. He recognizes these two. The one on his left is Special Agent Jake Halperin, and on his right is Special Agent Paul Loring. After watching and listening to them banter during more than an hour of footage while they searched his New York City brownstone, he feels like he knows them.

Sid looks left and studies Halperin's tense expression. The agent is staring ahead, at the back of the front passenger seat. His eyes are ice blue and moving back and forth as if he is searching for something. His face is clean shaven, his jaw is jutting, and a vein in his neck is pulsing. His hair is buzzed down to stubs.

"Stop staring at me, asshole," Halperin whispers through stiff lips and without looking at him.

Sid looks past him, out the window of the Suburban, and sees that some of the plain-clothes officers had their handguns drawn. He supposes they don't really know if he is dangerous. They would know there was a warrant for his arrest about a year and a half earlier. They'd know there was a manhunt for him. They'd know he was apprehended, but that he walked and was cleared. They would also know he has a handgun permit back in New York State.

"Am I under arrest?"

"Save it," says the agent in the front passenger seat. This one is older than the others. He has his tie noose tight under the white collar of his shirt, and his gray suit has the sheen suits get when they are worn and dry cleaned until they are nearly ready to fall apart at the seams.

"Where are we going?"

"You'll find out," says Halperin, still without glancing at Sid.

None of the agents look at him or say another word.

The silence is intimidating, but it doesn't last long. They pull into a parking garage under the Federal Bureau of Investigation's boxy headquarters off Pennsylvania Avenue.

Sid is dropped on his stomach on a blue carpet in a small conference room in the basement. Fluorescent lights are flickering overhead. A smell of old food and stale air is in the carpet. Special agents are standing over him with dour expressions. From the floor, he can see their bland black shoes. He feels hands on him and hears them breathing and pushing into each other as their fingers search from his ankles to his hair.

"This guy is wired up like a Christmas tree," says Loring.

Hands pull at wires leading from his belt to a camera pretending to be a shirt button and another in the pocket square in his breast pocket.

"This pen is a microphone," Halperin says. "Who do you think you are, Inspector Gadget?"

A third agent, a woman, carries the devices quietly out of the room and comes right back, shaking her head. His handcuffs are unlocked and jerked off of his wrists. Still lying on his stomach, his suit jacket is peeled off backward, and he hears its seams ripping. Hands reach around him to unbutton his dress shirt, but then Halperin impatiently rips it off, yanking his arms back. The shirt buttons make *pop, pop, pops*. Then his belt and shoes are pulled off. His socks and boxers go next.

His clothes are piled on a table in the room, and the female agent professionally searches them. He is naked now, his right cheek on the carpet, its stiff bristles scratching his skin as he looks up at her. She doesn't look at him directly. She is maybe five foot one, with red hair tied back in a ponytail, and a ruddy complexion. He recognizes her from the video in his home. In fact, he recognizes all three special agents in the room.

Loring orders him to get up and stand against a wall in the back of the small room. He does so casually, trying to act as if being naked here in front of these three agents in this room at FBI HQ is all some small inconvenience. He is turned around and around as a flashlight searches every part of him. While this happens, the two male agents are laughing lightly.

"Rubber-glove treatment time," says Loring.

"You never should have recorded and gone public with what we were saying when we tossed your New York place," Halperin says.

"Dumb move," Loring adds.

"When do I get my Miranda warning?" Sid asks loudly. "When do I get to phone my attorney?"

Halperin chuckles. "Don't you know the *Deep State* has the upper hand?" He says "Deep State" likes it's an inside joke.

"Huh, 'Deep State,'" says Loring. "Yeah, this guy is obsessed with the 'Deep State.' Well, I guess you could say we're pretty *deep* guys, McDaniel. We've dug deep into your background. And now, legally, *you're* in deep—very deep."

"He's an arrogant bastard," Halperin says. "See that little smirk on his face? This guy thinks he's big, bigger than the government. But he's not so big. Look at the little pecker he's got."

"Shut up," says the female agent who has been searching Sid's clothes. She is running a handheld device, looking for signals. It goes beeping mad when it touches Sid's left shoe. She picks it up and shakes it. Then she grips the black Oxford's heel and twists it. It comes off and a small device falls out. The female agent carries the electronic device quietly out of the room.

When she returns, she says, "You idiots, he was live-streaming audio of this. Everything you said was being transmitted to someone." Her outrage falls like cold rain over the room. She looks directly at Sid, who is standing naked with his hands at his sides and his back against a wall.

He doesn't smile. He doesn't blush. He doesn't try to cover up. He just cocks his head to the side and looks intently into her blue eyes.

She breaks eye contact and turns away, then asks, annoyance in her voice, "Do you have any other devices here?"

He doesn't answer. She glances at him but quickly turns away again.

All three agents look at each other and then at Sid. their expressions hard as cinder blocks. They know they could be in trouble. He had asked for his attorney.

Not a word is spoken after this, but the locker-room atmosphere is gone. Now, with the electronics gone, they are even rougher. Sid tries not to make a sound. He doesn't frown, wince, or threaten. He doesn't crack a joke or throw an elbow. He just calmly does as he is told. His ears and cheeks and his nostrils are looked into. Devices are used to search beneath his skin. He is turned, his balls are raised, and a flashlight searches behind them and over every other inch of his body.

He submits to the indignity passively.

Someone else enters the room and he is told to bend over the table so this person can reach up into him with rubber gloves. He feels fingers feeling around inside of him. The pain makes his eyes water. He wants to lash out. He tries to meditate. He breathes deeply and relaxes his body. The hand finally comes out.

The agents back away from him. He turns around and leans against the table and looks at them intently, as if he is trying to remember their faces or, perhaps, to look deep into their eyes, minds, and hearts. They look away.

He is trying to appear in control, to show they can do this to him, but they can't touch him inside. But inside, he is not so composed. He is livid and repressing thoughts of revenge. He is consciously relaxing his facial muscles, his shoulders and hands. He keeps his composure by forcing himself to think of these agents as people with families, with brothers, sisters, fathers, and mothers. Thinking of them as the complex people they are, as human beings with all the shortcomings people have, helps. It doesn't allow him to turn these people into monsters, despite their gross invasion of his body, of his sanctity as a human being.

No, he'll save his wrath for the monster telling these agents what to do. Yes, he'll wait for him.

The female agent still won't look at him. He studies her closely. He wonders what she had to do to gain this position, and what she still must put up with to keep her special agent status among so many men and a few very strong women.

He watches her as she packs up the devices she has used in a bag and carefully buckles it closed. She then turns and carries it out of the room without looking back at him.

After she has left, Halperin asks contemptuously, "Don't you even mind this?"

Sid smiles softly without showing any teeth, shrugs, looks at him, and says, "There is a time for everything."

The two young special agents frown, not sure what to make of this answer.

"You can put your clothes back on," Loring says.

Sid dresses slowly and with care to show he has dignity left. The two agents stand and stare at him. They look confused. The shorter agent, Loring, appears particularly insecure and nervous. So boastful and cocky one moment, but then, in the face of quiet confidence, they become rattled, unsure of what to do. A bully might keep going, but Loring isn't acting like a bully. The other though, Halperin—yes, he has the glare, insecurity, and demeanor of a bully.

"Oh, did we rip your fancy suit?" he sneers.

Sid looks at him and says, "No problem. I have many more."

Halperin steps close. "I am a federal agent with the FBI, not some traitor in custom suits the Russians pay for."

Sid watches this agent's cold blue eyes and knows this is just the type of guy he once had to fight on playgrounds.

When he finishes buttoning the few buttons left on his shirt, he asks, again with a calm tone, "So what am I being charged with?"

Halperin shrugs and says, "I am not the investigating agent. And anyway, that's up to the Department of Justice."

"So why am I here?" He glances around. This isn't a sophisticated interrogation room. He doesn't even see a camera. It looks like a small, windowless conference room, maybe for low-level government employees to eat lunch in.

"Just get dressed," says Loring.

As he pulls on his torn suit jacket, Sid says, "I would like to contact my attorney."

The two agents don't answer this time. That decision is apparently above their pay grade. They just wait until he is dressed, then they cuff his hands behind his back again and help him into a chair behind the conference table.

He looks at them and smiles. "You realize you won't get away with this."

That gets under Halperin's skin. "We're just getting started with you," he says with disdain heavy in his voice. Halperin is projecting the fragile aura of a bully about to do something mean in a vain attempt to fill in a hole within himself. Sid notices that Loring is watching Halperin, nervous.

Sid goads Halperin with a broader grin, then winks at him.

The agent takes a step forward, but stops himself as Loring says, "Jake."

Loring steps in, places a hand on Halperin's shoulder, and says softly, in a practiced way he has clearly had to do many times, "Down, boy."

Halperin backs up a step, his eyes still on Sid's. Then he and his partner walk out of the room and the door slams.

An hour passes slowly in the confines of the stale little room. Sid is still in the chair behind the conference table, listening to the office move outside the wooden door. One of the fluorescent lights is still flickering overhead. The others are all giving that cold white light. He doesn't see any cameras. Sure, cameras are easy to hide with today's tiny circuitry, but he doesn't know why they would go through the trouble to hide cameras in here. Why not just have some government-issue security camera right out there where it can be seen? He looks for likely places where they might hide one and his eyes settle on an air vent. There could be one up there, or in the wall for that matter, but this is hardly a standard interrogation room.

He hears feet clumping on tile. The door opens and a man strides in and slams the door behind him. He has short, dark hair laced with silver, a widow's peak, and blue eyes set behind deep lines cutting his thin, self-righteous face. He moves to the table and glowers down at him. He has his hands on his hips and a look of outrage in the hard creases of his smug face.

"How did you arrange this?" this man almost shouts.

"How?" Sid asks.

The man places his hands on the conference table between them and leans closer. His tie is clipped to his blue shirt, his jacket is off, and his shirt sleeves are rolled up. It's late in the evening now, and this man has had too much stress and coffee.

"There is suddenly video of you out there kicking one of the Russian agents we deported."

"How inconvenient for you."

The man straightens. "There is also video and photos of our agents," he says, struggling to put his voice under control. "That's illegal."

"Yes, that is really inconvenient all around." Sid's casual tone makes the man's face redden.

"We're taking all the video down. We've directed Twitter and Facebook and other social media to delete it. This footage of yours won't get you anywhere. The networks sure aren't going to touch it."

"Come on, Kuntz, you're chief of the FBI's Counterespionage Section, and surely you know better than that."

"So, you know me by sight," Neil Kuntz says, trying to suppress his surprise.

"Yes. And I thought the Chief of the FBI's Counterespionage Section would be smarter than this."

"What are you talking about?"

"That video will live forever on various sites and on the Dark Web. And that will erode your thin narrative, because you have decided to leak a lie and then try to hide it by playing censor. You can't get away with that in this wide open, digital age."

"No," says Kuntz with a snarl. "Twitter and the rest have to take it down and are now blocking anyone who tries to tweet a link to it. We could get them on espionage. It shows our agents. We control the news."

"Espionage? You control the news? Come on Kuntz, this isn't China."

Sid stares at him as someone does at a curious animal in a zoo. Neil Kuntz has one of those late-middle-aged mouths that's framed by two deep creases. Sometimes this merely accentuates a smile or frown, but in Kuntz's case, it is as if a pouty, unhappy, sour look was frozen into his face. Sid finds this expression deeply intriguing. It is as if Kuntz was cast to be a cliché of the Washington bureaucracy.

"And how did you get all of those reporters there?" says Kuntz. "I mean, you got two major news networks to show up. This situation might have been easier if you hadn't made your arrest so public."

Sid somehow keeps his poker face. He wants to ask what the hell Kuntz is talking about, but he swallows those thoughts and doubts. *He* didn't call in the press to document his arrest. This doesn't make any sense. If Kuntz and his team here didn't arrange that, then who did?

He tries to bury these questions for now. He can't let Kuntz know he wasn't behind it. So he breathes deeply and closely inspects the lines on Kuntz's face. As his mind clears, he tries to see the next chess move. He is close to being checkmated. And, if Adam is right, Kuntz and the FBI have a program here for choosing and controlling presidents that they can't allow to be exposed. Killing him, even taking care of his whole team in one way or another, are real possibilities.

"Do you even know what was on that flash drive the Russians tried to give you?" asks Kuntz.

"How would I know? I kicked him when he tried to hand it to me."

"We picked it up."

"Yes, I have seen the video," says Sid, playing dumb, for now. If Adam is right, he can't give Kuntz any clue that he is on to this secret "Vet the President" FBI program. "And I heard your agents say on the video I didn't touch it. One of them actually said, 'Damn, we almost had him.'"

"We'll arrest your whole team," says Kuntz. "We'll make them rot in cells. We'll get them with—"

"With what, perjury traps?"

"Fuck you."

"And gag orders?"

"This is Top Secret stuff."

"That won't stick. Media outlets that are leaked this thing can publish with First Amendment protection—the Pentagon Papers all over again."

Kuntz backs up a step, with the disgusted expression of someone looking down at a rat squirming for its crafty little life in the metal jaws of a trap.

"You're gonna have to make a deal," says Kuntz in a low, practiced, methodical tone. "And part of that deal will be an agreement that all of this video goes away, and you go away. That's the deal. You agree to a gag order for national security reasons, and you give us access to everything, to all of your accounts."

Sid realizes this is why Kuntz came to see him in person. He wanted to threaten his way to this deal. The video changed everything. Someone, maybe the FBI director himself, has kicked Kuntz's ass for how he has handled this, and now Kuntz is here to handle Sid, to make him quietly go away.

The idea is intriguing, but it might be too late. The game is afoot, and he has been arrested in public. If he doesn't clear his name, Sid's quiet business with America's Fortune 500 companies will dry up, as they'll be afraid of drawing too much government attention. The SEC, IRS, DOJ, and more—all have to be dealt with periodically by these companies, and they wouldn't want any undue attention because they have Sid's company on their books.

No, he has to clear himself. And he needs to do it publicly. He just has to be careful. He has no real proof of Adam's claims. No one is on the record. And the foreign government sources involved in this, like the ones in China, Russia, and Ukraine, are hardly going to fly on over to testify before a congressional committee: that would be a death sentence for them.

"If you'll exonerate me publicly, with a press conference, I think that could be arranged," says Sid.

"Like hell. We have plenty on you. You'd be wise to take the deal. You need to open up everything to us, to cooperate completely, and you need to do it now."

"That's not a deal. I haven't heard you give me any legal protection or anything I can show my clients. You could simply renege tomorrow and charge me with whatever you're drumming up. I'd be in limbo, knowing you could suck me into the legal system any time you find it politically convenient to do so."

Kuntz grabs the back of a chair and rocks it back and forth on its legs as he considers his next words. "For starters," he says, "we have information that you had contact with a known Russian complex in Maryland. But we don't want to press that. We don't want to strain relations with the Russians any further than we already have, at least for now."

Sid, his hands still cuffed behind his back, leans forward, stares hard into Neil Kuntz's gray eyes, and says, "I reported those *contacts* with the Russians to the FBI. I even mentioned it on a cable news show. I was tracing hacking attempts into American corporations. The hunt led me there."

"Good luck explaining that," says Kuntz. "You'd have to reveal the companies you were working for to prove that narrative, but you won't do that. You signed agreements with those companies that you'd never mention them in public. We know that, because you always sign agreements like that. And you make them sign agreements with you—agreements we can make those corporate wimps break any time with subpoenas. They don't want to run afoul of us."

Sid leans back and lets out a long breath.

"Make this deal and we'll let you go away—after we're satisfied," says Kuntz, still rocking the chair back and forth on its legs.

Sid notices the nervousness from the high-ranking FBI official's revealing face. He wonders if Kuntz looked like this as a child, or if, over time, his personality cemented into this petulant look.

"You've embarrassed us," Kuntz goes on, "but we can handle that. You haven't been dumb enough to release the 'Dirty Document,' so maybe there is hope for you. The document wasn't on any of the hardware we seized from your residences. But your attorney declined to give us access to your cloud accounts. We need that. We need your contacts. We need to know who you spoke with when you helped with the background on the dossier. We need to know everything before we can let you go."

Sid manages to keep his poker face, but he is confused. *What does he mean I wasn't dumb enough to release it?* Instead of asking this, he says, "Tell me about the accounts you're referring to, and we'll see. We want to help any legitimate investigation."

Kuntz stops rocking the chair and thumps his fist on the table between them.

"You must know we can do a lot more than embarrass you. We also have evidence that you've spoken to many of the people, including the Russian who gave most of the secondhand information for the dossier. You contacted this Russian three years ago when you were working on a case for a Wall Street bank. Parts of the bank were locked up in a ransomware attack. They wanted to pay, and though you recommended they wait, they insisted you contact the Russians responsible for the attack and arrange the payment to them. Maybe you didn't know it or maybe you did, but the person you spoke to in that encrypted call was in Washington, working for the Beckings Institute. He is a Ukrainian-born Russian named Sergey Dochenko. Soon after, as he knew we were watching him, he fled the country."

"Guilt by association, huh?"

"It's enough. You're all wrapped up in this web of people, and we need to know what else you have. The media will destroy you and your business for us. Take the deal. I can have documents for you to sign this evening."

Sid feels his hands in the tight cuffs behind his back. He pulls at them by flexing his shoulders to pull his arms back and his hands apart against the hard steel.

"I need to see my attorney," says Sid. "We'll discuss this and our other options."

"Other options?"

"I am a U.S. citizen, and we are in America. You can't try me secretly in court or hand me to another government. You can suppress evidence with Top Secret claims. You can stall and hide behind national security claims. But our government is too porous to keep all of this in. And my team has already gotten a lot we can use to counter your leaks and misinformation."

The deep fissures in Kuntz's face flex and loosen into a childish pout. "We haven't charged you with anything yet, but when your attorney shows, we'll let her see you."

Kuntz stands still for a long silent moment. "You're messing with the wrong guy," he says finally.

"No," says Sid, "I think you are precisely the guy I am here to mess with."

Kuntz begins to say something, but stifles the words. He turns, opens the door, walks out, and slams it behind him.

Just ten minutes later, he hears voices in the hallway. The door opens, and this time Kuntz is with U.S. Attorney Steve Jacobs and a young man Sid doesn't know. They pause just outside the door.

"Why hello, Steve," Sid says. "It is a pleasure to see you again." He looks at the young man, who is in a t-shirt, chinos, and white Nikes. "Who is your friend?"

All three walk in and close the door. There are only two other chairs. They exchange glances uncomfortably. Kuntz shrugs and points; Jacobs sits down and pushes the other chair to the young man. Kuntz stands behind them with his arms crossed and a deep Grinch scowl.

Hands still cuffed behind his back, Sid crosses his legs and smiles.

"I told you this wouldn't go well for you," says Jacobs.

Sid shrugs. "I need walking papers. A legal document that clears me. Something I can show to my employers to give them assurance I am still the trustworthy contractor I have always been. After that, I'll let your NSA snoops see what they need to see."

Jacobs looks back at Kuntz, but he still has his arms crossed and his eyes locked on Sid.

A long moment of silence settles over the room. Sid guesses what is probably on their minds. As is usually the case, all of them expect him to keep talking—to start rationalizing and looking for common ground and, as he does, to let things slip out. He doesn't. When the silence becomes too awkward, Jacobs says, "Aren't you going to say something?"

"Such as?"

"Such as, telling us about your involvement here, so we can make a legal determination of what we can do."

"Tell me more about what I should do. I'm fascinated," says Sid.

Jacobs sighs and glances at the man in the t-shirt. The young man's hair is over his ears, and he has tattoos on his arms. His blue t-shirt has yellow letters saying, "Forget Lab Safety, I Want Superpowers."

Jacobs continues. "We can make a favorable deal if you'll play ball."

"Ball?"

"We need access to all your accounts. To everything. And we need you to talk. To be honest and on the record. We need you to cooperate fully before we can clear you."

"Before?"

"We can use subpoenas, you know?"

"Then, why don't you? I've told you what I need. The next move is yours."

Jacobs sits back and glances up at Kuntz, who looks both angry and anxious. Jacobs turns back to Sid and uses his hands for emphasis as he says, "This will be much easier for you if you do this goodwill gesture first."

"What is it you're looking for?"

Kuntz snaps, "First, we want to know who gave you the dossier; next, we need to know everyone you sent it to. We know Gary Samson didn't leak this. We have total access to his system. So, if not you, who did?"

Sid laughs heartily, surprising them. "Is that why this NSA chap is here? To get passwords to my alleged accounts so you can do a forensic analysis of my team's online activities?"

"How did you—" the young man begins.

"You are in the typical NSA-geek costume," Sid interrupts.

"Are you going to deal?" asks Jacobs.

"For what?"

"Your freedom."

"You haven't charged me with anything. All you can do is hold me for seventy-two hours without charging me, and you can only hold me that long if you allege I am a terrorist or something. If you do charge me, it'll be grand jury time, and that gives me a lot of legal options."

"You are an online terrorist," says Kuntz.

Jacobs holds a hand up to Kuntz and says to Sid, "Come on. Who sent you the, ah, Dirty Document, and who did you send it to?"

Sid wants to say he doesn't know, as he has not been able to source the encrypted email. It came with a warning that he is involved, but it came through proxies, remailers. He spent days trying to source the document. He found Global Positions quickly. From there it meant hacking them and doing a computer-forensics search of their system. He found Gary Sampson's accounts to be surprisingly easy to hack. Social media entries showed him to be obsessed with growing another inch, so Sid sent him in an email with an ad for tall-heeled cowboy boots. When Samson took the bait and clicked on the ad, it downloaded a program. The website he was sent to was fake, but another click and it seamlessly sent him to a real boot maker, so Samson had no idea he'd been phished. Getting his email passwords was then easy, as he keeps them in a contacts file on his hard drive. Before long Sid had administrative access to Global Position's network. He found the contacts he needed there. A lot of what he found is the same information Adam followed to the web of informants the president's son, Buck, also used for his pay-for-access schemes.

Still, he knows better than to give a clear answer to any question these three might ask, especially without his attorney present.

Anyway, he is puzzled. He thought that maybe they had leaked parts of this document to harm or control the current president. If they aren't doing that, who is?

At this point in the game, he actually does need something from them: something that'll clear his name—a legal document absolving him that would have to be carefully written, agreed upon, and signed. It would have to be good enough to hold up in a court.

The other way out is with these officials' heads on a public platter. He doesn't see any way just yet to accomplish that, but these Deep State goons are very scared of something. This puts him in a very vulnerable position, and he just doesn't know enough to play to a stalemate, let alone to checkmate.

"I have asked three times now for my attorney. I am now asking again. I want to speak with my attorney."

"We're told she is coming," Kuntz says coldly.

"What is it you are so scared of?" asks Sid while looking at Kuntz, knowing this will push them out of the room.

All three of them look at each other, then back at him. They don't say another word as they file out.

Hours pass. The chair is hard, his hands hurt, and his bladder is aching. He knows someone is outside the door. He can hear the person's feet moving now and then on the tile. He swallows the urge to complain, but he knows he'll have to give in to his body before long.

He is considering shouting when the door opens. Agent Stephanie Baker steps in and closes the door softly behind her. She leans back against the door for a moment and takes in his appearance: his ripped-and-rumpled suit, his dress shirt with missing buttons, his hands cuffed behind him. She then nods as if she just made a decision and steps across the room to take a chair on the other side of the small table.

Her blonde hair is tied back and up, and her expression is neutral on her makeup-free face. She is in dark slacks and a jacket. Her shirt is gray, and she is not even wearing any perfume.

"I knew you'd end up here," she says. "But you did look really cool on that electric bike."

He smiles. Yes, he likes her. She is marvelous. She is in control of herself, and he is becoming very aware of all the dimensions of the part she is playing.

"Are you here to offer me a deal—hopefully in a kinder way than Kuntz did?"

She clasps her hands together, looks down at them on the table, then back up into Sid's eyes. "Yes, that is why I was sent in here."

"I'm sensing a *but*."

She actually smiles, then draws back, places her hands on her slacks and rubs her thighs nervously. "I observed that meeting you had with the Russians."

"I know. We have you on video."

"Yes, I saw your team member—Jorge, I believe—a few cars over from me."

Now Sid leans back, confused. Why hadn't she told her bosses? Or had she? His eyes ask her this, and she says, "Our orders were to observe."

He nods, but is still confused.

"Those orders have changed," she adds.

He nods again.

"But"—she stops and stares at her hands again before looking back up at him—"I saw the footage *they* released." She shakes her head and is quiet. Sid can see she has a lot she wants to tell him, but that she won't, not now.

They hold each other's eyes, trying to see in, to understand each other. He knows there is now a lot between them that needn't be said. He is pleased to learn her team is not communicating everything to Kuntz. If they had, Kuntz certainly would not have leaked the video of Sid with the Russians. He would have known there was likely other video that could come out.

"Are we under surveillance? I don't see a camera."

She shakes her head, touches her chest, and says, "No, it is malfunctioning."

He smiles, nods, and says, "I don't need you to be a whistleblower. You'd have to go to the FBI's Inspector General, who would report your claim to senior members, including Kuntz. They would simply ship you to a field office in Fargo or something."

She just stares at him. Something in her eyes tells him the ground under her—all of her patriotism, her years of law school, and then at the FBI's Training Academy at Quantico, Virginia, endeavoring to earn this role in her country's government—feels as if it is shaking.

"We both know the federal bureaucracy destroys whistleblowers," says Sid. "But I might, someday, ask you to testify. If that happens, all I ask is that you be what you are now, and have been: one of the many, many honest and good members of the FBI who understand that American freedom is not an impediment to your agency, but that it is exactly what you have raised your right hand to swear to protect."

She smiles, showing her perfect big, white teeth. She clearly likes him, or maybe she is just amused by him. She sinks farther into her chair as her shoulders relax and she says, "I heard you were an idealist."

Sid smiles, says, "I'm an idealist who needs a bathroom."

CHAPTER

10

The hallway down to the bathroom is eerily empty on this subterranean floor. The door is kept open by a Special Agent Paul Loring's foot and, when he is done, Sid's hands are cuffed behind his back again and he is taken to the small conference room.

After dropping him into a plastic chair, the two young agents leave the room. The door is closed, and there is the click of a lock. He hears one of them sit on a chair just outside the door as the other joshes, "You want a book or something, Jake?"

"Fuck you," says Special Agent Jake Halperin.

Sid gets out of the chair and sits on the carpeted floor. He brings his knees in to his chest and rolls back as he tries to pull his handcuffed arms down over his hips, then past his knees and feet. He barely manages it and almost laughs. Even this small victory is worth celebrating.

With his arms now in front of him, he lies on the brown carpet in the back of the conference room. He can hear air moving in the ductwork above. He hears little noises in the building, muffled sounds of chairs moving and elevators going up and down. He tunes it out and focuses on relaxing his toes, then his ankles, then his calves before his quads, then his back and on up his body, until his entire muscular system has let the stress and discomfort fade away. He focuses on nothing, the void, an almost empty, white moving thing, like a cloud somewhere up in an otherwise clear sky, and then he falls asleep.

Sometime early Thursday morning—he thinks, but isn't sure in this windowless confine—Loring and Halperin return. This time, they are visibly unhappy to find him resting so peacefully on the carpeted floor with his hands on his stomach and a pleasant smile on his face.

Halperin kneels, grabs his wrists, and pulls hard to make the metal cuffs bite into them. He uncuffs him, and they pull him to his feet.

Sid ignores the rough treatment, yawns, stretches, and says, "Good morning."

The two agents pull his hands behind him and cuff them behind his back again. They then yank him by the arms above the elbows, out of the room and down a hall toward an elevator. He asks for a bathroom, and Loring says, "Yeah, all right."

He is taken to the same small bathroom along the hall, uncuffed, and allowed to go with the door once again held open by Loring's foot.

After this, his hands are cuffed behind his back again, and he is led to the elevator and up to the third floor. They step off and go down a long hall past offices, most of which are empty at this early hour. He is guided into a large conference room. This one has a long table, swivel chairs, and a window showing that the sun is up on a bright morning.

Gloria is seated behind the conference-room table, her thoughts cloaked in her beautiful, expressionless face. She is in a black suit. Her dark hair is down over her shoulders. Her black-rimmed reading glasses are halfway down her Italian nose. Her legs are crossed. She looks well slept and amused. She smiles at Sid, and her eyes twinkle. She waits for the pair of agents to leave and the door to close before she speaks.

"They are not supposed to be recording this—attorney-client privilege and all that—but they probably are." Her brown eyes flit to little dark covers that hide cameras in two places on the ceiling.

Sid nods, sits on the floor, and pulls his knees in again to bring his cuffed hands over his feet and in front of him.

Gloria watches this yoga move and says, "You look like you've done that a few times now."

"Yes, I wasn't sure if I could do it the first time. But it made all the difference. Do you have a paperclip?"

"Sure." She reaches into her briefcase and finds one in a side pocket.

Sid takes it and sits in a chair across from her. Using both hands, he bends the paperclip straight and then pushes an end of the wire into a hole in the handcuffs. He uses the hole to bend the paperclip into a "Z" shape, then inserts it into the keyhole on the cuffs. Gloria watches with her fingers clasped together and her brown eyes intently fixed on Sid's hands. He fiddles with the make-shift key for a moment before the locking device disengages and the cuff falls off his left hand. In a moment, he does the same for his right, and the cuffs clang onto the table. He then rubs his wrists, looks up at her, and gives her his best boyish smile.

"Old hacker gag," he says. "In school, we used to see who could do it fastest."

"So you have always been like this. Heartening."

Sid shrugs and looks down at his torn shirt and suit jacket, and the destroyed shoes. His suit is wrinkled, the shirt is partly untucked, and so many buttons are missing that part of his stomach is showing.

"Keep you up all night?"

"Oh, no," says Sid pleasantly, "I got a few hours on a carpet in a basement-level conference room."

She smiles, showing all her white teeth, and says, "No one plays the game the way you are, Sid."

"Maybe that is why I am playing it this way."

Gloria re-crosses her legs, shakes her head, and gives him that *tsk-tsk* look she does when someone is being naughty. "Even Edward Snowden had the sense to leave the country."

"Right, but the difference is, I didn't do anything—they've planted evidence, and now they're trying to play a guilt-by-association game with me."

"Least they can do."

"I thought they just liked perjury traps."

"We'll try to stay out of that minefield," she says.

"Well, it would be a sort of hero's journey to be a whistleblower. I think I'd stand up and take it all right."

"And smile patriotically as you get it Sir Thomas More style, huh?"

Sid rubs his wrists. "Is that coffee?"

She pushes a paper cup across the long table to him. He uses both hands to take its lid off and carefully raises the steaming dark liquid to his lips.

"It's getting a lot of play," says Gloria, "even though it keeps disappearing."

"What is?" He slowly puts the coffee cup down on the table.

"The full-length recording of you kicking that Russian."

"Oh that. Well, it got me some fun treatment last night."

"Live-streaming your arrest and the beginning of their interrogation of you was stupid."

Sid wonders if he did go too far, but then, they never did read him his Miranda rights.

"Was it in your shoes?" she asks.

"One of them was."

"You're such a naughty spy."

"No, don't ever call me a spy," says Sid as he takes another sip of the hot coffee. "That insinuates I work for some government. I don't, and I never have or will. I work for private corporations and individuals, and I only take the jobs I want."

"Well, you sure use the tools of a spy."

"Fair enough. I need the tools to nab those doing corporate espionage."

"And our government—you did use those tools against them."

"That's fair too," says Sid as he takes a deep breath and looks around the forgettable room. "But I wasn't working for a government. I was, well, what did Henry David Thoreau call it? Civil disobedience. Anyway, I didn't do any setups. I only recorded and went public with what they decided to do at my brownstone, at my cabin, and to me here."

"Stop justifying."

"Just trying to figure it out, I guess," says Sid.

"That kick you gave to the Russian agent—his name is Igor—was it fun?"

"Now you're teasing me. That's good."

"What does this win you?" she asks.

"Them."

"I didn't think you were so self-righteously idealistic."

"Maybe I am. I think I'm just mad, though. I don't like being treated like this."

"You asked for it."

Sid sips his coffee again before saying, "Funny, I don't mind this rough treatment. Well, other than the rubber glove thing—which I didn't know was a real thing—it's all been a small inconvenience. But the way someone here at G-man Central made me a part of this dossier, to give it authenticity at the expense of my reputation, my business, and freedom, is too much for an American to take. They should have left me alone."

Gloria shakes her head. "You keep saying 'they' like some conspiracy nut would about black helicopters."

His head feels heavy and weary. Maybe he isn't thinking rationally.

"I don't want to be here. I want to be living my life. Doing the work I do and escaping when I need to. But they decided to suck me into this."

"So it is all about your pride. All government personnel aren't plotting, Deep State goons, you know. Most are good people doing hard, thankless jobs. Oh, most enjoy it, or at least like it; they aren't martyrs. They are well-paid and pensioned employees. But they are normal people, Sid, not the Gestapo."

He gives her a "come on, please" look.

"Sorry, Sid," she says, reading his disappointed expression. "I know you don't think like that."

"Right. I've met enough FBI agents to know they are good, smart people doing complex investigations. I have a lot of respect for them—most of them. So much respect that I am doing this, in part, for them."

"So, what's this about then?"

"It's about taking out the few who aren't. It's about shedding a bright light on a small team who tried to use their power to change an election—this time by not letting the American people know something. It's about cleansing the system, something that has to be done every so often, I suppose. If the republic is to last."

"I see. This is a morality play. You're cast as the hero, a defender of the republic, a true citizen standing up to the machine that, not too long ago, tried to destroy an administration—and now, it seems, is working to protect another one by hiding the truth, and maybe destroying you in the process." She raises a brow. "It doesn't add up, Sidney."

Sid sighs. "Yeah, there is something I'm missing. And you're right, it sounds grandiose, I know. But look, this is what I do. I just usually do this quietly for international corporations. I clean them of bad actors. Now I am trying to do this job for my government—without pay, even. Maybe this is penance for having been given so much by the American system."

"Okay, let's get down to business," says Gloria. "They have you on a lot of small stuff and some big stuff. It is not legal to secretly record federal authorities and then to go public with the recordings. Now, the stuff in the parking garage is easy to defend. You are a journalist. That was a publicly accessible place. But the audio of the interrogation, such as it was, that you live-streamed is another thing. Still, they never read you your rights and haven't charged you with anything yet, so we have plenty of legal room to push back there, too. Same with the recordings from your home and office, but they can make a lot of trouble."

Sid starts thinking out loud. "I do want to play a strictly legal game, but it is hard when they make the rules and give themselves all of the exemptions. Anyway, it was live-streamed out to foreign cloud accounts that others have access to. Someone else made it public."

"With your permission."

"No. Those are semi-open accounts. It's like a buffet for a party. And it was done in places without treaties allowing the American government access. I won't tell them who else has access. I have the First Amendment right to deny them that. I am not even sure of everyone who has access. It is a vetted list, but not centrally vetted. It's more of an unsigned agreement between cyber friends to only let in the right people. Our government can't get that data, and they can't make me take it down. It is not even in my control now. It's out there on the Dark Web and on places a Google search should turn up. They can keep scrubbing the public-domain sites, but there really isn't anything they can do to completely censor it."

"Permission was implied," says Gloria.

"Yes, it was."

Gloria scrunches her lips and pushes back her hair as she thinks. Her brown eyes are bright and alive, but her voice is uncertain as she says, "This is vague, new stuff, Sidney. Who knows how a judge will rule, as it was recorded here. Judges are old people who don't understand this new world. Few really do."

"Some in the NSA do," says Sid, letting his mind wander around the Washington landscape. "Most in the government don't. Many laws are getting hard to enforce, but they don't see it. Their response is to assert more control, yet the system, the technology, is ahead of them and it's getting easier for everyone to use. The federal government fought Pretty Good Privacy—the first real, publicly available encryption. The State Department actually labelled it as illegal 'munitions.' *Munitions* of all things. It took a First Amendment check—Phil Zimmermann put the code into a book and published it back in the 1990s—to use old First Amendment law to protect how these rights are used today. The genie has since escaped the bottle. The government keeps trying to hold back time, but they can't. Meanwhile, their attention should be on another place entirely. If they don't realize that soon, they're going to miss things bigger than the nineteen hijackers on 9/11. So I am actually doing them a big favor. I am dragging them into the new, emerging world."

"We're not killing a bottle of wine in your Manhattan office right now, Sidney. We're at FBI HQ, and we need a plan," says Gloria. "So let's get specific. They're going to charge you."

"I doubt it."

"*Huh?*"

"That would mean a grand jury, discovery, and court hearings. Look, the Department of Justice won't want possible court decisions that would result from taking this to a constitutional challenge. They don't want to deal with the Freedom of Information Act requests that would result from all that courtroom stuff. This team here, the rogue elements in it, certainly don't want a public investigation. This little cabal of individuals doesn't want sunlight, so right now they're panicking, trying to find a way out."

"So?"

"Kuntz offered me a deal. He wants me to shut up and go away—not much of a deal, really. My name would still be suspect, which would be a cancer to my business, but they do want me to go away very badly. He had a lot of fear in his pouty face when he personally delivered his proposal."

Gloria laughs, and it's a genuine, big laugh. "Yes, it is a weasel's face—or is that too unkind to weasels, which can be a little cute? Maybe it's a rat's face. Yes, that works all around. Kuntz has the face of a rat."

She glances at the dark cone hiding a camera and smiles.

Sid is pleased to see she is joking about this.

"Are you willing to take the deal for a little more?"

"Yes," says Sid, "I told him I want them to put out a press release stating that I am not under investigation, that I have cooperated fully, and that I am not being charged with anything, as they have found no evidence of any wrongdoing."

Gloria again glances furtively at one of the dark cones on the ceiling hiding a video camera and then back to Sid who is simply sipping his coffee. "Okay?" she says in the long, drawn-out way people do when they are both surprised and unsure what to say.

Sid puts down the coffee, leans over the table toward Gloria as he motions her closer with a wave of his fingers, and whispers just loud enough to be overheard, "If they don't give us that deal, as soon as you leave this building, have the team initiate Operation Total Release. I want everything, I mean everything, out."

Sid sits back into his chair.

Gloria's eyes are glassy, and her body stiffens. She says, "This is how you want to play it?"

Sid nods and winks.

"Well, I'm glad I had a full breakfast and that I wore comfortable shoes." She pushes her dark hair back out of her face as she dramatically lets a pen drop from her hand onto the table.

CHAPTER 11

Special agents Halperin and Loring enter the conference room and stop and stiffen with anger. From his chair at the table, Sid looks back at them pleasantly.

Their eyes go from Sid's smile, to the wooden conference table where the handcuffs lay open and empty of Sid's wrists, then harshly back up to his eyes.

He spreads his hands in mock apology. "They were getting a little uncomfortable."

"Get up," says Halperin.

"Has Gloria—ah, that is, my attorney—come to an arrangement with you?"

"Get up."

Sid stands.

Both agents are white, young, serious, clean-shaven, with similar noses and cheekbones, and they seem to always have matching expressions. He takes in their buzz cuts, their rigid jawlines, their dark, square-fitting suits and dark ties against white shirts. He looks into their judgmental, cold blue eyes, full of disapproval of something they clearly don't understand.

They are twenty-something men trying to hide their inexperience in stern demeanors. They are both the sons of politicians.

He can tell they are trying, but failing, to hide what they really think of him. They are looking down at this Sid McDaniel character from their special agent status, and they see him as a wannabe cop, a hacker who is paid way too much Wall Street money to mess around in foreign affairs. Their glares are censorious, but also unsure. An older cop can pull off the dead face, the uncaring expression of someone who has seen too much. But these just-out-of-college FBI agents haven't yet learned to let their disdain sink beneath their flesh and deep into their hearts, where it can turn them cold to blood on the pavement and to crying widows and to young men in trouble, men they could have been like if one or two things had been different.

"We're letting you walk," says Halperin before adding, "for now. Your attorney is still upstairs."

"Already? You can legally keep me here without charging me for seventy-two hours."

"Oh, have you enjoyed your stay?"

"Hotel FBI leaves much to be desired. Dare I say the detention facility might have been more accommodating."

Loring rolls his eyes.

Sid turns to the shorter agent. "Given that they are a congressman and a state senator, both of your fathers must be happy you have the FBI on your resumés. Be great for when you run for office," says Sid.

The young man's eyes tighten.

"Okay, Paul Loring and Jake Halperin, let's go. I could use some lunch." Sid walks past them and stops in the quiet hallway on this subterranean floor.

Loring hustles to catch up. "How do you know our—?"

"You were both in my Uptown place. You both admired my suits—though, Jake, you did call me a 'rich shit.' Yes, I have audio and video of you both in my home, and of everyone else who served that warrant and invaded my brownstone and my cabin. Given what I do for a living, I'm wondering why you're feigning surprise that I've checked you out? You do know I investigate people for a living, right?"

Halperin steps out of the room, puts his right hand on the center of Sid's back, and pushes him like a high school bully would. Sid shrugs and starts to walk. They go down the hall to the elevator. Halperin hits the button, it lights up, and they wait in silence. Halperin has his hands on his hips and is rocking from his toes to his heels. Neither of them is looking at Sid. They are clearly annoyed with his release. When the door dings and opens, Halperin again pushes Sid in, and then they stand on his left and right, like two bouncers walking a belligerent drunk out of a club.

When the elevator doors shut, Halperin leans close to Sid's ear and says, in a half-whisper, "I want you to know, you are not going to put my face out there again. I saw the video clips of me you put online as I searched your fucking New York City place. That's not right. I am not going to let you fuck my future. I hope you get what I mean. I am not fooling around."

Sid listens to this hissing threat, but doesn't give Halperin the satisfaction of a glance. As he stares at the elevator door, he says, "Even FBI agents are accountable for their actions."

"You're fucking with the wrong guy's life right now," Halperin snarls as the elevator doors open.

"Oh, when you run for your daddy's seat in Congress, don't worry—you can just explain that what you said to me was only locker-room talk."

Halperin shoves Sid out into the hallway, causing him to bump into a woman with files in her arms. She stumbles and almost drops them, and Sid puts his hand under the files to prevent them from falling to the floor.

She says, "Thank you," but then sees his missing buttons, torn suit, rumpled hair, and the special agents behind him, and she scurries off.

They march on either side of him down the hall toward bright light coming in an entrance. There is a metal detector and a few Capitol Hill Police officers in uniform.

When they reach the officers, Sid is told to sign out. He finds this odd, as he was never asked to sign in. He does so and is given back his wallet and keys, his pen, and his pocketknife. He asks, "Where are my phones and other devices?"

"What other devices?" says Loring.

"Oh, I see."

"Anything we took will be returned to you eventually."

"Eventually?"

"They are subject to the active search warrant."

"Are you going to follow me around taking my phones whenever it might please you?"

"If we want to," says Halperin, as his eyes add, *Fuck off, we're in charge of you.*

In a moment, Sid is through security, and walking out alone in his rumpled and torn suit, into a sunny and warm morning on the streets of the nation's capital.

Without a phone, he can't even call an Uber. He starts to walk east down E Street. It's nearly two miles to his motorcycle, among hurrying people in professional clothes, along gray sidewalks beside busy streets, but it passes fast as he stretches out his stride. He sees the Capitol dome on his right, down New Jersey Avenue past the National Japanese American Memorial. He stops and watches the people around him every so often. He is looking for anyone following him, for anything. Nothing.

He thinks of the spare phone he keeps in a small, locked compartment on his motorcycle. He picks up his pace and passes Union Station under the spring-green trees near Columbus Circle.

Two blocks from Union Station, beside townhomes stacked elegantly along a fashionable side street, he reaches his bike. He punches in a code to unlock a tiny compartment that looks like part of the seat, pulls tape off a battery attached to its back, and turns the phone on. His first call is to Jorge. It goes right to voicemail. Same for Adam and Gloria.

He doesn't bother to leave messages. He knows they've been detained.

He scans the bike and smiles when he detects the FBI tracking device he left under the seat. He'd forgotten about the little tattletale that'll tell the government everywhere he goes. He looks over the bike more closely and doesn't see anything else. He has a weird feeling about this, about being left alone out here. In jail they could do anything to him, even turn off the cameras and hang him, like they did to Jeffrey Epstein.

So why did they let me walk?

He thinks about this as he sits on his bike and looks up and down the quiet street. A young woman jogs by. A man in a suit opens a front door down the street, closes it, locks it carefully, and walks gingerly to a waiting Uber. Seems like a normal morning on this upscale street in the spring sun.

Maybe there aren't that many of them? This question teases him. In a prison they'd need to trust a warden, and enough guards to take care of him there. That could be problematic for them. Even in FBI HQ, he'd mostly been handled by two green agents who'd been handpicked and groomed for this.

Out here on the street, they could take care of him in a few different ways, if they wanted to. Or maybe he is just not that important, now. After all, he doesn't have anything they don't—as far as they know, anyway. Would they take him out, just to make sure? Maybe they would, just to be certain he doesn't keep investigating this thing. His profession is to forensically dig into the digital details for the truth and then to expose the bad actors, including whoever hired them. But, still, he doesn't expect a Jason Bourne-style hit. That would lead to too many conspiracies, the unraveling of which could lead to exactly what they want to hide.

No, they'll need something more believable, something with context, with a narrative built in.

He touches the Safari icon on his iPhone's screen and Googles himself as he sits on the bike in the warm sun.

"Shit!"

His name is everywhere. Kuntz has been busy. Stories have been planted and info leaked widely across the media landscape.

That reporter who sat on his couch during the raid of his Uptown place has a story up, quoting an "anonymous source" saying Sid is "a depressed, Uptown tech kid with erratic behavior who, maybe for attention, has his digital fingerprints all over this libelous, so-called 'Dirty Document.'" This reporter also has photos of old letters—letters from old girlfriends left in a box in his cabin—to back up the point. He also has emails and text messages and other things. All obvious leaks from the FBI. They've only leaked parts of them, segments that make him seem overly emotional, maybe unstable, since love letters—or worse, Dear John letters—are never really rational.

Why didn't I throw those letters away? Nostalgia could be the end of me.

There are also photos of Sid in various disguises while he was undercover. *Did the FBI take these?* The article cites an FBI profiler who suggests this may be evidence of a "psychological disorder" that is perhaps "schizophrenic." The profiler insinuates that perhaps Sid needs professional help, that he might even need to be "committed involuntarily."

He scans rapidly through other articles that quote competing cyber firms who, without names attached, call Sid "unbalanced" and "a man who has the delusion that he is a cross between 007 and Bill Gates." One tech CEO opines that Sid, and his column *Solam Veritatem*, push the narrative that he's a nonpartisan truth-teller, but that "his involvement in this 'Dirty Document' proves that to be sanctimonious bunk." Several articles say Sid secretly planted false information; they cite "high-ranking government sources" who say the information, or disinformation, likely came from Russian and Chinese sources, and from operatives with agendas of sowing misinformation designed to stir up partisans.

None of the articles even mentions the data he linked to in his column, data that backs his innocence. Also, none of them mention the audio and video released of the FBI teams in his home and cabin, and the audio he streamed of his arrest and the beginning of his interrogation—an interview the FBI kept trying to continue even though he kept asking for his attorney. Most don't even quote or link to the video of him outside the Dubliner. The few that do say only that he had to be apprehended for questioning pertaining to his alleged involvement in working with foreign sources to dig up dirt on the president.

It's classic kill-the-messenger stuff, with the added twist that Sid is unbalanced. He closes his eyes and takes some deep breaths to let anger out of his chest. "I didn't have anything to do with this 'Dirty Document.' This narrative is a complete fabrication," he mutters to himself aloud, like a madman.

But then, he worries, maybe he *did* have a hand in it—unintentionally. Gary Samson as much as said Sid's undercover work was used for part of it. Sid tries to recall cases over the past few years for anything that could be directly linked to this opposition-research document. He did investigate many of the people cited in it. He did business with the banks mentioned. He found and watched corporate spies from Russia and China and got them fired—though not prosecuted, as the companies didn't want attention that might affect their stock prices, and some of those people are connected to this dossier.

Unintentional or not, it wouldn't be difficult to make him appear all wrapped up in this.

No, they probably wouldn't murder him. But clearly, they are building a narrative that would make a suicide believable, even damned likely.

If that is to be their big move, then what move can he make to avoid being a "suicide"?

How can he also set them up?

He decides he needs a quiet and safe place to study the problem. He needs to see them coming and to have countermoves planned. He doesn't like having to wait for them to act, but he doesn't see a move he can take right now. Another column, of course, but even that will take planning, thinking about what to say and not to say. Telling people he is sane and that he'd never harm himself could just make him sound crazy.

Sid puts in passwords to link his phone to a cloud account that filters his various phone numbers. He then syncs the built-in Bluetooth in his motorcycle helmet to this iPhone. He checks the video cameras hidden on the bike by flipping them on with a switch installed near his left thumb.

He decides that riding will help clear his mind to show the path. The battery is low, but he has a little time for a ride.

He drops the phone in his suit's breast pocket, starts the bike, and lets its quiet electric motor take him up the little side street past the pretty townhomes in the late-morning sun. He turns left on Massachusetts, merges with traffic, and then right on Constitution at Stanton Park. He meanders by the Capitol Building and lets his mind run through every part of the dilemma.

He hears a beep, telling him a call is coming in, and reaches up to hit a button at the bottom of his helmet.

"You told me I'd know when to call you."

Carole's lovely voice.

Sid pulls out of traffic and stops in the shade of a tree on Delaware Avenue, across from the trees and flowers in Upper Senate Park.

"Yes, Carole?"

"Senator Haskins had me leak some things. *Um*, an FBI psych profile of you, for one. If it's real, I shouldn't even be talking to you, but—you just don't seem like this profile at all! I only read part of it, but...it makes you seem, well, *insane*. It says you 'likely suffer from a multiple personality disorder.' Sid, that's not all. They're leaking that you hacked Top Secret stuff. They talk a lot about your contacts with Russian and Chinese operatives—people who, they say, are likely spies. They don't just imply that you're selling information; they say you likely are, and they talk about various foreign bank accounts to back up the point."

"Carole."

"Yes?"

"Do you really believe any of that?"

She doesn't hesitate. "No. That's why I'm telling you."

"Thank you. What phone are you calling me from?"

"The one you gave me."

"Good," says Sid. "You'll need a paper clip. Push it into the hole next to the SIM tray and remove the SIM card. Destroy the card—use a cigarette lighter, if you can. Then wrap the phone in a lunch bag or something and throw it in a public trash can."

"*Um*, okay."

"This is about to get very hot, and I don't want you near me when they move again."

"Oh, Sid."

"I'll be in touch. After."

Sid hangs up but continues to sit in the shade, his mind whirling.

Why would Senator Richard Haskins, a politician known for protecting whistleblowers, be leaking twisted information like this? He understands the motivations guiding Kuntz and the others, and what they want to hide to protect a president who supports their agenda or to protect themselves, or he thinks he does, but he doesn't understand this. None of this is adding up. He decides he needs to read the "Dirty Document" again and to follow its sources and where they lead a lot more closely. He just hasn't had time to dig deep. The first few times he read its fifty-one pages, he was entirely concerned with why and how he was added to this thing. But now, with Adam's new revelations and what Carole just told him, he needs to do a deep dive.

Sid starts his motorcycle and pulls away from the Russell Senate Building, letting the electric bike move slowly under the trees along the edge of Lower Senate Park within Washington's stately façade.

He tries to calm himself by looking at the trimmed trees and the simple and refined classical buildings. This city is austere, stoic, as simple as a man's suit. He likes that. Washington is the clothes on a man, just as Paris is the bright evening gown on a lady. Washington walks like a man. It sticks its chin out like a man. It is stoic and juvenile like a man. It lives on power and stupidity and ego like a man. No one really understands Washington, as most men don't completely understand themselves. No one controls Washington—not the 435 members of the House or the 100 senators or the president or all his cabinet members or other officials and certainly not the media.

So, who does? With Adam's information on this Deep State method of choosing and controlling presidents, it looks so different. Maybe there are controls outside of the Constitution and the elected officials. Maybe the deeper controls are held by the self-righteous, self-important, and increasingly corrupt players in the U.S. intelligence agencies. They have all of the information. In this new digital age, they have everything they need to quietly take control. They could easily use that information to control elected officials, even if it were just to control them a little here, and a little there, to pad their budgets and their power. He lets out a long breath. *Is this real, or am I becoming a fucking conspiracy nut?*

He continues on, meandering aimlessly down the streets.

Whether or not this is an empty conspiracy theory, the real situation, or some combination of the two, he doesn't want to be destroyed by this town and its officials as they look to protect their power. He realizes this was inevitable, given his occupation. For years, he has been investigating international corporate spies from China and Russia. Many of them are also connected to American think tanks here in Washington, to American tech firms, or to U.S. academic institutions. They also often rub elbows with the moneyed class of influencers who affect the legislation. It's all a big, sticky web, and he has been playing in it, getting wealthy in it, for nearly a decade. He shouldn't be surprised that a spider in the web wants to eat him.

He catches sight of the white Capitol dome again, dazzling in the sun. Beneath Washington's granite and marble façade, its well-established culture was once guided by gentlemanly laws and norms. Everything is accepted in this town that doesn't make a public spectacle or kick the status quo in the groin. It is easier to go along with Capitol Hill culture than to buck its unwritten rules. This is part of the reason why so many outsiders are baffled when a maverick, a real Mr. Smith Goes to Washington type, arrives in D.C. and quickly morphs into just another Washington politician, one earmark and altered position at a time. The culture here is oppressive, and it will protect itself.

But these deeper things, this power held and used by intelligence agencies, is the frightening tip of the spear. It could turn America into a police state, a place with centralized power controlled by a few, instead of a federal system with checks and balances.

He thinks about the United States Foreign Intelligence Surveillance Court (FISA) and pictures the judges who serve on it. He considers what the Foreign Intelligence Surveillance Act empowers them to do. They are supposed to be a check on the government, but have long acted as a rubber stamp. When they are asked to approve requests for surveillance warrants on foreign spies inside the United States, they say yes more than ninety-nine percent of the time. The judges on the FISA Court are afraid not to trust the officials from the agencies that ask for these secret warrants. They've okayed a lot of warrants on partial or false information that has then allowed the FBI to legally spy on American political figures.

Even as this digital age has brought unbelievable freedom of expression, it is also bringing an Orwellian opportunity for control of the populace through what information people are allowed to see and communicate.

He is pausing at a traffic light. A large cloud has passed over the sun, chilling the air.

He feels overwhelmed.

"All of this is too damned big! How do I walk away clean after swimming in this swamp?"

He has said it aloud, almost a shout, and even with the visor on his helmet down, his voice is loud enough to startle a young couple walking past him on the sidewalk. Their reaction makes Sid laugh at himself, a good laugh that lets out some of his mad tension. He shakes his head, looks over his right shoulder, and gives the bike a little juice.

I need another column. I need to counter the character assassination they just put out there.... Should I write about the rubber-glove treatment I got last night? Yes, don't leave anything out. Be honest. Be open. People turn away from someone who is hiding parts of a story from them. They really appreciate the complete truth, when they can get it. It's refreshing. It's refreshing because it is so unusual today.

Then he thinks: *Maybe I should drop by Senator Haskins's home tonight.*

He knows the senator lives in a townhome not far from the Pentagon, and only a ten-minute walk from the townhome his team has rented for the month. Maybe in person, and away from Capitol Hill, Haskins will level with him. Maybe he can learn why the senator would leak a nasty FBI psych profile of him to the media.

Haskins just can't be in cahoots with Kuntz and the others. That doesn't add up. His public record is someone who protects whistleblowers.

But then, such a public image would be great cover for someone helping the Deep State choose and control presidents. The intel agencies like such operators, people who appear to be one plain sort of thing, but are really the opposite.

Senator Rich Haskins is chairman of the Senate Intelligence Committee, after all. He could be very useful to people like Neil Kuntz.

He accelerates, squinting against the sun that just emerged from behind the cloud.

CHAPTER

12

Moving in traffic now, Sid feels almost calm in the storm of his dilemma. The sky has turned gray in the late afternoon, and raindrops from a spring shower start peppering the visor. Inside the helmet he is listening to the smooth melody of "Stay Alive" by Jose Gonzalez while drifting with traffic on Route 395 toward Virginia, to the townhome they rented. From there, he hopes, he can at least see them coming.

The gray skies, rain, window wipers, and car lights behind him make Sid tighten his grip a little on the bike. As the soft melody ends, he enters a tunnel leading to the Fourteenth Street Bridge over the Potomac River to Virginia. Tunnel lights are softly glowing above, and he keeps his eyes on the red taillights ahead.

Deep in the tunnel, he just sees a flash of a sedan changing lanes on his right, coming blurry fast toward him. A person in a car might not respond so abruptly to the aggressive move from another motorist, but someone experienced on a motorcycle knows that drivers in autos who make fast turns or who don't look enough before changing lanes might only dent or crack the plastic panels on their cars, but that the person on the motorcycle might just become an organ donor. He pivots his weight hard to the left and accelerates with all the fast bike can give him, and the car just misses his back tire.

The sedan is just behind him now and still coming aggressively. All he can see in his mirrors are its headlights in the tunnel.

This bike is rigged with six cameras he can flip on and off with a button by his left thumb. It's a package designed by a film prop company located in Brooklyn. One camera is just under the headlight, another under the taillight. One is alongside each foot, another is on his helmet, and a fifth is where the gas tank would be on a gas-powered street bike. This last one gives video of the rider, as is required to be a social-media star. Sid has no interest in the social-media showoff applications, but, as a security specialist, he likes the possibilities all these cameras provide.

With a flick of his left thumb, Sid turns on the bike's video cameras, which begin to livestream his ride to various accounts. Red taillights ahead are coming fast, but he doesn't slow down with the car closing in behind him. Instead, he shifts his weight and darts between the cars ahead by driving right on the dotted white line. He hears a crash behind him as the pursuing sedan smashes into the backs of both cars on his right and left. The sedan slides into the far left lane.

Sid shifts his weight and moves the motorcycle to the far right of the four lanes and hides behind a truck. He watches the sedan pull ahead of him on the far left, so he slows and moves back into the center lanes to come around behind the sedan. As they emerge from the tunnel onto the bridge, he pulls right behind the tan sedan. He then shoots up beside it, driving outside the white line to look in at the driver who just tried to run him down.

Sid brakes next to the driver's side window but sees only a part of a face in sunglasses and a Washington Nationals baseball cap. But the man's jawline and nose look familiar.

"Halperin," Sid mutters to himself.

The sedan's window is closed. The driver is looking at a smartphone in a holder attached to an air vent to his right. The phone's screen shows the sedan as an icon of a blue car now going over the blue Potomac. It also shows a flashing red dot that must be the tracking device on Sid's motorcycle, right next to the blue icon.

When Halperin sees where the motorcycle is, he jerks his head left and sees Sid looking in at him from three feet away.

He yanks the wheel left in another attempt to knock Sid off his motorcycle.

But Sid anticipates the move and brakes hard. The sedan just misses him and slaps against the cement barrier along the bridge, throwing sparks, before rebounding back into the far-left lane.

Sid is now following a couple of car lengths behind and making certain his cameras get the sedan's D.C. license plate, with the "No Taxation without Representation" slogan.

He reaches under the bike's seat, finds the tracking device by feel, and pulls the magnetic device off.

Just as he does this, Halperin cuts right, forcing a dozen autos in front of Sid to brake hard in the now-pouring rain. The sedan crosses three lanes of traffic as cars swerve to avoid it. An SUV slides into two others. Several more can't stop and bang into the SUV with loud, metallic thuds. Sid brakes and veers right; his motorcycle slides on the wet bridge, and he just manages to get around to the right of the colliding autos. He skids to a stop against the back of a blue SUV in the far lane.

Ahead, the sedan scrapes against another car as it makes a ramp on the right onto the George Washington Memorial Parkway.

Sid slaps the tracking device to the back of the blue SUV, then maneuvers his bike between the SUV and the right-hand cement barrier as other autos are still thumping into each other in the rain behind him. He follows Halperin down the ramp onto the George Washington Memorial Parkway. The FBI agent's car is way ahead now and going fast into the taillights and rain. Sid leans low as he accelerates and tries to keep vehicles between himself and the sedan.

Halperin takes a left exit to Washington Boulevard, goes around a traffic circle, and takes the Arlington Memorial Bridge back into Washington.

Sid follows from as far behind as he dares. They go past the Vietnam Veteran's Memorial and onto Constitution Avenue. As he tails the sedan, Sid is shouting in his helmet a narration for the video.

"I'm in pursuit of a driver who looks to be an FBI agent named Jake Halperin. He just tried to run me down, and now he is trying to get away from me. He is in a four-door sedan, and I am on an Arc Vector street bike."

The sedan has slowed now and is flowing with traffic. The gray sky is unleashing a torrent of rain, and drivers have their lights on and wipers on high. Halperin takes several turns, moving away from the heart of the capital. Sid keeps up his running monologue as he stays a half block behind.

"Jake Halperin, a special agent with the FBI, is running from the scene of multiple accidents he caused on the Fourteenth Street Bridge. He is now meandering through Washington, possibly looking for a good place to dump his unmarked car."

Up ahead Halperin takes a hard right at a red light onto North Capital Street. There is some traffic, but he accelerates and changes lanes as he snakes between cars. He has a green light across H Street and keeps going.

The light at K Street is red, and he runs it by turning right. He is still going a little fast, but he stops at the next light at First Street. Sid sneaks behind a van a block back and waits. Sid is staying far behind now, risking losing him as he hides in the traffic. When the light changes, Halperin stays straight through a tunnel beneath the train tracks leading to Union Station and turns left on Second Street.

When Sid makes the same turn, he doesn't see the sedan. He stands high on his motorcycle as he passes a Fresh Farm Market at Second and L, then stops alongside an active construction area.

Sid's mind is racing.

What am I doing? I'm chasing an FBI agent. What would I even do if I caught him?

He wants more video, but this is insane. He is almost glad that he lost him when he sees a flash of a car the right color turning off L onto Congress Street. He follows. At the corner of Congress and L, he slows and peeks down the dead-end street running behind a Sherwin Williams Paint center and other brick buildings. He sees Jake making a three-point turn a block down the alley, then start to parallel park into an empty space, facing him.

Sid has a decision to make. Should he wait to get video of Halperin walking out and maybe engage him on video?

No, I need video of him in the car.

He takes a deep breath, turns left on Congress and slowly, as a man would approach a bull in an arena, glides down the middle of the dead-end street. He stops twenty feet away. Halperin doesn't notice; he is looking the other way, behind him, backing the damaged sedan into a parking space, between a Volkswagen Mini and an old Dodge Charger. He begins to use the sleeve of his suit jacket to wipe down the steering wheel.

Sid raises the visor on his helmet. Rain drops wet his face as he watches. Then he yells, "Hello, Jake!"

The agent stops wiping down the wheel and looks up from beneath his red-white-and-blue Washington Nationals cap. He freezes at the sight of Sid sitting there, staring at him.

On his sleek, black motorcycle, facing this enemy in the pouring rain, in the center of the dead-end street, Sid suddenly feels like a cowboy in an old Western, awaiting the bad guy for the shootout scene.

Jake's knuckles tighten as he grips the steering wheel, and his lips tighten against his teeth. He knows he has been made. His ballcap and aviator sunglasses aren't enough of a disguise. He also knows McDaniel's bike is loaded with cameras. There was some debate in the office about whether to disable them or to take them, per the search warrant, but the consensus was it wasn't necessary. They wanted to follow him, not tip him off that they'd messed with his bike.

Yes, he's being filmed.

There is a long pause as they stare at each other. McDaniel's visor is up. Jake hates that Sid looks like he's smiling at him.

Jake doesn't know what to do. He sees his future slipping away. He has political aspirations. With the FBI on his record, and help from this program and from his father, he could rise high. But with a scandal on his record, if all of this goes public—especially with audio and video of him committing crimes—he wouldn't have a chance. At best, his career would dead end. At worst, he might end up in jail.

As those thoughts race through his mind, he hears the bastard saying, "Meet Jake Halperin, the special agent with the Federal

Bureau of Investigation who just tried to run me down in the street. Apparently, I am too much of a threat for this crew in the upper-echelon of the FBI to allow to live. I know too much, and this man is my would-be assassin."

That does it. There's no other way out. He must take this cyber punk down.

Jake looks around. Just scraggly-looking trees and parked cars and red brick buildings and a dead end. No one in sight.

He turns back to Sid and feels hatred well up again for this so-called "cyber hunter," who has gotten rich hacking international corporations and government agencies. This unpatriotic parasite has enough information to do real harm to this great nation, and he must be stopped.

With this decision made, Jake starts the car. With the vehicle in park, he mashes the gas pedal. Its engine roaring, he throws the car into drive.

The front end of the sedan clips the rear end of the Volkswagen Mini parked in front of it, shattering its taillight, and the car surges out of the parking spot with a glass-shattering growl and high-pitched squeal of tires. The auto lurches and skids to right itself.

Sid doesn't move, doesn't even flinch for a few nanoseconds of slow-motion time. He is suddenly a matador without a cape. He knows dodging while drawing the bull means waiting to the last possible second.

The car leaps at him through the rain. He sees Halperin's evil grin as he leans over the wheel. He knows that maniacal face is being caught on multiple cameras on his helmet and bike, and streamed live to Facebook and other sites.

Then, in just the instant before impact, Sid rolls off the motorcycle between and under the cars parked on his right.

The move is so late that Halperin makes the mistake of swerving to follow Sid's movement. The sedan's airbags deploy as it smashes into a parked red Toyota Sequoia. Glass shatters and showers onto Sid, now flat against the pavement on his stomach while the Sequoia rocks and convulses above him.

The sedan's front end is up on the back of the Sequoia, crushing its rear window, and its right rear tire sits atop the now-destroyed motorcycle.

Sid hears a sound like garbage bags being opened. Sid pushes with his hands on the asphalt, sliding feet first out from under the Sequoia and a white Honda Civic parked right behind it. Rising, he sees the noise is Halperin fighting the white inflated airbags, trying to squirm out of the shattered driver's side window.

Still wearing his motorcycle helmet, Sid purposely steps up to the window and points its video camera at Halperin. His head and part of his shoulders are clear as he contorts his body to get out. His nose is busted, and bright red blood is flowing over his mouth and chin. A SIG P320 is in his wildly flailing left hand as he desperately tries to squirm out of the still-running car. Noxious-smelling radiator fluid is spilling over the hot engine and pooling on the pavement.

Sid grabs Halperin's left hand and twists the gun toward the agent's thumb, prying the pistol from his grip. It drops on the shattered glass covering the wet asphalt. Sid then pulls Halperin out of the car by the arm and neck. When he slides out, Sid transitions to a wristlock to take him all the way to the ground. Halperin lands hard on his left shoulder and yelps. He rolls free of the wristlock by rolling toward it. Then he bends his left knee and claws with his right hand to get a backup pistol in an ankle holster.

Seeing what the agent is attempting, Sid grabs his right wrist and twists while pulling the hand back. In the same motion, Sid uses his left hand to grab the pistol from the ankle holster. When he has the gun, he lets go, stands, and tosses the micro-pistol into the sedan's backseat.

Halperin is lying on the broken glass now, glaring up at Sid. He moves his legs and feels the SIG Sauer that Sid knocked out of his hand under his left leg. He reaches fast for this gun.

But Sid steps on Halperin's right arm, pushing it into the dull shards of glass covering the asphalt. He picks up the Sig, pushes the release to drop its magazine, and pulls back the slide to eject the round in the chamber. He then also tosses the gun into the back seat of the still-running sedan.

"You'll pay for this," Jake gasps, his face wet from blood and rain.

"For what?"

"For everything."

"For not letting you run me down with this car?"

"Fuck you," says Halperin, who suddenly lurches up, grabbing Sid by the waist. Pushing his bloody face into Sid's chest, he drives forward with his legs, slamming him back into the parked Civic.

Sid gasps as the tall agent continues to drive his right shoulder into his chest. He grabs Halperin by the shoulders and drives his right knee into his chest.

Halperin grunts, then pulls back to gain leverage and smash Sid into the Civic again. He is too strong for Sid to hold. The man rams his shoulder into Sid once more, smashing his back into the Civic. Sid grunts in pain as he feels the front window frame on his spine. He reaches down Halperin's body and pulls his suit jacket up and over his head, as a hockey player will do in a fight on the ice.

The FBI agent pulls back again, but this time Sid goes with him by holding onto the suit jacket. As Halperin tries to straighten, Sid changes his grip to the man's ears and headbutts him with the top of the motorcycle helmet, smashing the video camera but knocking Halperin unconscious.

Sid lets go, and the agent falls backward to the wet pavement. He lies still, the rain washing his still-bleeding face.

People are running down the street now. Some are shouting.

"You okay?"

Sid pulls off his helmet. "Yeah, but I'm not so sure about him. Please call 9-1 1. We need an ambulance and the police."

Sid leans over the man, who is lying on his left side, almost in a fetal position. He searches the inside pockets of his suit jacket and finds a wallet. Inside is a badge and ID that reads Special Agent Jake Halperin, Federal Bureau of Investigation. He finds a phone in another pocket.

He stands up.

"Hey man, whatcha doin'?" says a middle-aged man in a t-shirt and jeans as he kneels down beside Halperin. "Maybe you'd better turn that car off."

Sid nods and reaches in past the mostly deflated airbag and turns the key in the ignition, shutting off the engine.

More people surround them and begin asking Sid if he is okay. He waves them off and looks at the agent's phone. As he flicks the map screen away, the phone starts to ring a Darth Vader ringtone.

The screen reads, "Neil Kuntz."

Well, well.

He taps the screen. "Yes, sir."

"Jake, where are you?"

"Parked down a dead-end street."

"What have you done?"

"Only what I was told."

"What you were told? We had a fucking plan," says Kuntz.

"I saw a chance."

"A chance? You aren't supposed to think. How many times do I have to tell you? This needs to be handled quietly. Shit, politicians' spoiled kids are such morons."

"What should I do now?"

"Dump the car. Clean it. We'll have a team there. Looks like Sidney McDaniel is out in Virginia now. He is still on the move. We'll need to…um…look, get your ass back here. I have another call coming in."

Kuntz hangs up, leaving Sid shaking his head in the rain and almost laughing. He has to admit it, a good part of the reason he is playing the game this way is it is so damn fun. But then he shakes off the amusement as he realizes there isn't much time to enjoy this in the present tense.

He works fast to airdrop the phone's contact list, its text messages, voicemails, and photos to his phone, which automatically updates them into his cloud accounts.

He hears the sirens just as he finishes. He needs time to think, to look at everything he just downloaded, but he only has moments.

CHAPTER

13

Waiting feels stupid, but running so much worse. There are a dozen people now around the crash, and sirens are a few blocks away as the rain shower begins to taper off. He hopes he'll get a trial. In a trial there is opportunity, even if you're up against the U.S. intelligence agency apparatus.

Sid turns around and puts his hands on the Honda. He looks at his reflection in its passenger-side window. His hair is flattened down from the helmet and is now soaking wet. His pale blue eyes look washed-out and weary. What's left of his white dress shirt is smeared with the blood of an FBI agent. He can see his skin through it as it sticks to his chest. His ripped suit jacket is now brown with street grime from sliding on the pavement under the Sequoia.

He has the look of a man on the run.

He turns around to look over the scene. He sees the sedan with its wheel on his motorcycle and its front end up on the red Sequoia and all the people trying to help an FBI agent. He notices that at least six of them are using their phones to take video. And he sees a man in a t-shirt and jeans holding Halperin's head up while trying not to get blood on himself. The face looks like someone beat it with a hammer, and he tries to soothe himself with the fact that fresh blood from a face wound will make a person look like that. But he sees that Jake is coming around.

Sid looks back at the phone in his hand. Now that it has updated to the Cloud, with a few flicks of his thumb, he uses the iPhone's "Erase All Content and Settings" function to clean its hard drive. It's a tool designed for those who want to sell their phones, but everyone knows it's also a function used by tech-savvy people who think they're about to be arrested.

He then dials his attorney's number. As Gloria's phone rings, he watches Halperin's eyes fluttering open. He sighs and waits, resigning himself for what's to come. Gloria's phone goes to voicemail.

"Gloria, I am about to be arrested again. Make all the necessary inquiries."

Fifteen feet away across the tight street, Jake's eyes blink, then focus on him.

Sid kneels and slides his phone under the car, to his motorcycle.

The rain has now completely stopped. Everything is wet and gray.

"You!" shouts Halperin as he tries to sit up. "You, you!" His voice is congested from congealing blood in his nasal passageway and mouth. His eyes are bloodshot. Bruises are already starting to show around his nose and cheeks. He finally sits up and pushes people off of him.

Sid tosses the wallet and cellphone toward the man's feet. He squirms to grab them and, still on the ground, clenches the wallet and phone in his hands as his gruesome face squeezes into a grimace.

The baying sirens make the dead-end street, and the red brick walls around them echo in their deafening shriek and flash in synch with their lights.

When they arrive, their sirens go silent, but the lights from an ambulance and the two police cruisers continue to splash blue and red in the ally.

Halperin is pointing at Sid, now leaning back against the Civic.

"Him, him, arrest him. I'm Special Agent Jake Halperin. Arrest him."

Three officers draw their pistols and tell the dozen people to back up and clear the way for two EMTs in blue scrubs.

"I'm an agent with the FBI. Arrest him. He attacked me." He is holding up his ID.

Sid raises his hands, attracting the officers' attention, and causing people around him to back away. Several are still recording the scene with their phones.

"Turn around and place your hands on the vehicle."

Sid does so.

Hands touch his chest, waist, and legs. They take his wallet and keys. Then come around to his front and down to his groin. His hands are yanked back and handcuffs are snapped onto his wrists.

"You have the right to remain silent...."

A strong hand on his left arm pulls him away from the Civic and past the ambulance, guiding him down the now-crowded, dirty little street. Another hand on the back of his neck pushes him down into the back seat of a police cruiser. The door slams shut.

"I need medical attention," says Sid just as the door closes.

"You'll have to wait."

Sid slumps against the seat, closes his eyes, and breathes slowly. He tries to visualize what might happen next. He needs to mentally prepare. He needs to anticipate the coming moves so he can react correctly.

He decides he'll need to force the point that he needs medical attention. It is sure to be a lot more comfortable in a hospital room than a jail cell. He might even get a meal, even if it is hospital food.

He opens his eyes and asks himself how he got into all of this. His life for the past week has been a runaway freight train. He has been trying to think out his moves ahead of time, but maybe he has been acting too fast. He thought his best chance was fast chess, but now he isn't so sure. Maybe Gloria, David, and Jorge are right.

The scene around him feels so surreal. He feels a fool. Yeah, his team has been more right that he'd admit. He played this all wrong. Too fast and aggressive. These government goons hold all the cards. He should have made a deal, even a bad deal. He should have played the game instead of trying to transcend the game.

Another car pulls into the alley, doors open, and two men in dark suits step out. One is Paul Loring. The other is Neil Kuntz. He looks smaller here, outside. His buzzed-short gray hair, glasses, hard shoulders, the beginning of a pot belly, the scowl on bloodless lips, make him look so common.

"The fucking fool," he hears Kuntz say as they walk past the police cruiser.

Loring and Kuntz stop and stand over Halperin as an EMT cleans his face with wipes to assess the wounds. Loring's arms are spread wide in the classic "what the fuck" posture.

Halperin is shaking his head and looking at the ground. He looks like a man apologizing.

Kuntz shoos away the EMTs. When they're clear, he leans over the sitting agent and puts those bloodless lips near his left ear. Kuntz probably knows there is nothing more intimidating than an authority figure in your hierarchy leaning close to whisper in your ear what he is going to do to you. Halperin's body goes rigid, and his hands clench and unclench.

Kuntz waves at the EMTs to let them know they can go back to work. Then shows an ID to the officers in blue. Sid faintly hears him say, "We are in charge of this crime scene. Don't touch anything. Don't photograph anything. Our trucks will come to take away this car and this bike. What did you take off of this suspect?"

An officer hands over Sid's wallet and keys.

Halperin finally stands with Loring's help. He's holding a towel to his nose and nodding as his partner speaks.

Now Kuntz walks to the end of the alley with a phone to his ear. He stands in front of piled-up pallets and a car that looks like it was parked and left there years ago. He is listening, barely speaking now. After ten minutes, he puts the phone in a pocket of his gray, pin-striped jacket and slowly walks back to the other two agents.

They stand there talking and glancing at the cruiser with Sid in it for several minutes, as three officers watch with thumbs in their belts and the contented expressions of street cops at a lively crime scene on their faces.

Halperin breaks off and limps to the wrecked sedan. He manages to pull a backdoor open. He leans inside, searches around, and finds his carry gun and his backup pistol. Sid watches him put his foot up on a bumper and shove the pistol back in its ankle holster.

Then the trio walks over to the officers. They all laugh about something for about three minutes before the cops, followed by Kuntz and Loring, walk up to the police cruiser.

A key goes in the lock and the door is opened.

"Come on out."

Sid puts his feet out first, ducks his head, and gets out with the help of an officer's hand on his shoulder. Another turns him around and says, "These are my cuffs," then takes them off and pushes Sid toward Loring. "Your prisoner."

"I need medical attention," says Sid, and the two EMTs turn to listen.

Loring turns Sid around and pushes him over the cruiser's hood as he cuffs him again. As he does so, he leans close and says, "Oh, where does it hurt? Here?" And he digs his knuckles into Sid's spine.

"For starters."

The agent steps back. Halperin chuckles nervously. With the towel held to his nose, his laugh sounds like a child with a mouthful of milk. Kuntz looks hard at him, and he shuts right up.

Then Loring leads Sid up the street to an unmarked brown sedan. He opens the rear driver's-side door and orders, "Get in!"

Sid decides not to say anything more. He hopes there are too many witnesses here watching him enter these agents' custody for him to be in any danger. He notices that a few people are still recording the scene with their phones. He wonders if they know he just live-streamed the car chase, the hit-and-run, and the attempt to take his life in this dead-end street onto Facebook and various cloud accounts on the Dark Web.

He slides into the car and sits on his cuffed hands, and Loring shuts the door. Loring gets into the driver's seat, while Kuntz takes the passenger seat. Halperin gets in the back and sits beside Sid. He is still holding a towel to his face to stop the blood.

"You sure you don't want to go to the hospital, Jake?"

"Nah." He tilts his head back against the seat to slow the flow of blood. He isn't in charge now. Maybe he is even in trouble. Whatever the case, Jake Halperin has disengaged into a quiet, subservient role.

Loring starts the car and carefully backs out into the street.

"Am I under arrest?" asks Sid.

Neil Kuntz puts his left hand upon the back of the seat and turns his body to face Sid with his cold blue eyes.

"Not yet," he says.

"What does 'not yet' mean?"

"Did we read you your rights?"

"An officer did."

"Did we?"

"No."

"We're taking you back to your residence," says Kuntz with a steady, hard voice. "Consider yourself under informal house arrest until the Department of Justice decides what to charge you with."

"And what might that be?"

"You endangered the life of a federal agent. You pursued said agent across this nation's capital. You boxed him into an alley and threatened his life. You then impersonated a special agent of the FBI while speaking with his superior."

"He tried to run me down. I have that on video."

"No," says Kuntz. "I have seen the footage you live-streamed to Facebook. It shows you recklessly driving and leaving the scene of an accident on the Fourteenth Street Bridge. It shows you pull up in a threatening way on a federal agent. It shows you pursuing the agent by running red lights. It shows you breaking multiple traffic laws. It shows you aggressively trying to harm an FBI agent. It shows him, instead of using his firearm to end the threat you presented, simply trying to get away as he sought backup."

"Uh-huh," grunts Jake through the towel.

Sid sits back and closes his eyes. It's true he didn't get Jake's first attempt on his life on the video cameras. He didn't start the cameras until after that initial incident. He can also see how a lawyer could explain Jake's attempt to run him down in the ally as self-defense, even as someone trying to escape harm. Yes, he knows he screwed up—and that just might be checkmate.

He looks up at the buildings, all covered with the sheen of spring rain. He watches Washington, D.C. flash by, and he lets his eyes wander down to the people on the sidewalks and in their cars, all oblivious to this weird drama playing out in this boring brown sedan that has everything to do with the health of their federal government.

CHAPTER 14

The sedan stops at the back of a circle in a quiet cul-de-sac in front of the townhome Sid's team rented. Four unmarked cars and a van are in the small driveway and parked along the curb. Halperin gets out, angrily tosses the bloody towel onto the seat, and slams the door. As the other two get out, he circles behind the car, opens the door for Sid, and orders, "Get out."

Sid steps out and hands the handcuffs to him.

"Why, you son of a—"

"A paperclip. It's in my left back pocket if you want to try it yourself," says Sid.

Halperin steps in, but Kuntz barks, "Stand down, Jake."

The white front door of the townhome is wide open. Just inside, an FBI team is packing up bags on a tile floor at the base the stairs. They've obviously swept the place for DNA and fingerprints, and have searched for electronic devices to seize. They've likely left behind some bugs of their own. He wonders if they found all of his team's listening devices. He feels as if this is no longer his rented townhome. This is now an extension of their domain.

He is still soaked from the rain. His shirt is now dark with dried blood and so wet it is sticking to his chest. His chest and back hurt and his pants are brown with grime. But he looks reasonably decent compared to Jake's face.

"Guess we can see who won the fight," says one of the on-scene agents as he looks from Sid to Halperin, grinning.

"Fuck you," says Halperin.

"Can I order you guys a pizza?" Sid says to the nearby agents as he walks through the front door. He climbs the stairs to the living room on the second floor.

Kuntz is already there, and two other agents are just leaving. Kuntz has his hands on his hips, and the pouty lines on his face are even deeper. He sounds like an unhappy school teacher as he says, "Consider yourself under house arrest. You are not to leave this premises. If you need food, you can order it. We'll have agents out front and in back. As soon as the DOJ decides to arrest you formally, we'll bring you in. Right now you are considered an active national security threat. Sections 1021 and 1022 of the National Defense Authorization Act of 2012 give us the authority to temporarily hold you. We're being kind by keeping you here."

"You're a real angel," says Sid. "Mind if I go get a shower?"

"Not at all."

Sid walks past Neil and goes up another flight of stairs to the master bedroom on the third floor. He pulls off the tattered remnants of the suit he has been wearing for two days, tosses it in a bathroom trash can, and steps in front of a body-length mirror. He sees deep, black-and-brown bruises on his chest, touches them and feels the pain, but nothing seems to be broken. He can breathe all right. He hears the front door close downstairs as voices go outside, but he knows they left things behind to listen. He wonders again if they found all of his team's devices.

Showered, shaved, and dressed in jeans and a blue polo, with a bourbon in his left hand, he turns on a large TV that's attached to a wall in the living room. He puts on a cable news network and turns up the volume. Outside double glass doors and across a small patio, he sees a man in an overcoat leaning against a short brick wall that runs around the patio. The man has his hands in his pockets.

Sid puts the drink down on an end table and goes to the town-home's little elevator, which is just out of sight of the patio. He knows, even in a rental, it'll have telephone service, as it is the law in Virginia for elevators to have working landline telephones. He doubts the FBI noticed it, as it is too basic, too old-fashioned, but he unscrews the ends of the small, black phone to check for bugs. He doesn't see anything. He wishes he had his kit so he could sweep for signals, as they could have placed a device on top of the elevator or anywhere. Regardless, he must assume they've tapped the phone from outside. But then, maybe they didn't. All he and his team have used here have been cellphones. This is a new rental. The contract for this phone is taken care of by the leasing company that manages the property. Sid doesn't even have the phone number for this landline.

He puts his hand over the phone's receiver. He dials Gloria. It goes to voicemail. He tries Jorge. The same. He tries Adam. Nothing. He doesn't leave messages as he knows he'll be overheard. Instead, he dials a voice-messaging service he has used in the past. He doesn't have to speak to set up a new account. He uses the phone's keys to start the automated service. This overseas service records messages, transcribes them automatically, and sends them instantly as audio and text files to any email addresses or, as texts, to phone numbers attached to the account. He puts in various email addresses his team will check and pays for it with a temporary credit card number he has memorized. He then memorizes a short account number and new password. He uses associations for passwords and this time picks "72739-843-324" (Screw the FBI). He steps out of the elevator and closes the door most of the way.

He turns off the second-floor kitchen lights and sits at a table in the half-dark room with a sandwich and the bourbon neat, watching the front of the townhome from between the slats of wooden blinds. He sees a dark car with men in it. He also sees a van parked down the street. He is certain they'll come from the front.

It's nearly midnight and becoming Friday morning before he sees a black Lincoln Town Car coming slowly down the street. It stops at the curb in front of the townhome. The street is otherwise quiet.

Sid gets up from the kitchen table and walks to the elevator in the living room. He pushes open the door, picks up the elevator phone, dials in his account number and password to the messaging service, and sets it to record a message. He leaves the phone off the hook, closes the door most of the way, and walks back into the kitchen as he hears the front door opening.

The doorbell didn't ring. There wasn't a knock. The door just opens, and he hears feet clunking up the wood stairs. Four men in suits walk in.

Jake Halperin stops in the kitchen door and looks at Sid, who is still seated in a kitchen chair. He looks at Sid like someone might at a convicted murderer locked safely behind steel bars.

The other three search the place again. One goes upstairs and another downstairs. The third searches this floor. They have devices. They are sweeping for signals. Through the kitchen door and past Halperin's cold eyes, he sees the man in the living room turn off the TV. He then begins scanning. He finds something, pulls back a couch cushion to look, but then nods and carefully pushes the cushion back. He does this again at a built-in bookshelf opposite the TV in the living room. Sid shakes his head and smiles, knowing this agent is just finding their own bugs.

"Your nose looks better," he says, eyeing the medical tape holding Halperin's broken nose straight. "Don't let them set it too straight. A little crook in your nose will give your plain face some character. Maybe even a story to tell at those FBI get-togethers. Well, I guess you wouldn't tell them the truth about how it happened, but perhaps you have the creative capacity to make up something good."

He is trying to get a rise out of the man, but only manages to make him smile. It is a doozy of a smile though. Not an evil grin exactly. It's more like the grin of a cat that has cornered a rodent.

The three other agents come in behind Jake, and for a moment they are all standing together looking in the kitchen door at Sid, who is still seated at the kitchen table with a bottle of bourbon in front of him.

"I hope he's drunk," says a very large one.

"Doesn't matter," says Halperin.

"Okay," says an older one, who appears to be the senior agent on the scene, "let's get him in the living room. The kitchen is too close to the street."

One of the agents walks into the kitchen and stands behind Sid. This agent is very big. His brown eyes are cold, unkind. He has the look of a bouncer who is hoping for a fight with a drunk, unruly patron. This agent's black overcoat falls off his shoulders, doesn't touch his waist by six inches on either side, and stops at his knees. He says slowly, carefully enunciating each word, "Get up and go into the living room. Nice and easy, now. No kicks like you did to that dumb little Russian. I am not supposed to hurt you."

Sid stands and walks out of the kitchen into the large, open room. A dining room table that'll seat eight is on his left. The elevator is on his right just at the top of the stairs leading up from the front door. Beyond the elevator are two brown leather couches facing each other in front of a fireplace. Built-in bookshelves are on the right. A large flat-screen TV is up on the wall on the left. On both sides of the fireplace are double glass doors. The doors on the left open to a brick patio. The doors on the right open to a path of red pavement stones that lead out to a path connecting the back patios along the row of townhomes. After the path are trees. The woods rise up for 20 yards before falling down a steep hill to an apartment complex 50 yards below.

Sid hears a *clunk*. He turns and sees that Halperin just took a pistol in a clear plastic bag from a pocket of his overcoat and dropped it unceremoniously on the dining room table.

"Recognize it?" the agent asks.

"Looks like my SIG."

"I guess you're not stupid."

"No, but you are. I have a receipt for that pistol. I had my attorney get a receipt for everything you seized from my brownstone and from my cabin. Your department was very officious about it, actually. The receipt is dutifully stamped and includes the serial number, which matches the number on my pistol permit."

Halperin's eyes search the faces of the other agents in the room. His breathing is now a little faster, and his eyes are glassy.

"Screwed by the efficiency of your own bureaucracy," says Sid.

"We can produce another receipt," Halperin says stupidly.

"Really? That's your plan? You're going to say you returned the gun to me, a terrorism suspect, while I was in Virginia, so that I could shoot myself?"

The older agent sits down in a chair at the far end of the dining room table, looks at one of the agents Sid has never seen before, and gestures at the stairs. The other agent picks up the pistol in the clear plastic bag, walks out of the room, and goes down the stairs to the front door.

"Getting another gun, huh?"

"Have a seat," says the older agent.

Sid just rests his hands on the back of the chair.

"We don't have to do this. You just have to give us what we want."

"What is your name?" asks Sid.

"Special Agent in Charge Charles Mulham."

"And what is it you want?"

"You've been told that already. Access to everything. All your passwords to all your cloud accounts. All your encryption keys. Everything. Then we'll put you in a safe house while we search them. If we don't find anything illegal, you can walk. If we do, we'll charge you. Otherwise…" The agent shrugs.

"I commit suicide."

"That is up to you."

The fourth agent walks back up the stairs, reaches into his pocket, and places a snub-nose .38 revolver on the table. He quietly walks back down the stairs and out the door.

"Did you at least put hollow points in that .38?" asks Sid.

Halperin snorts through his broken nose. "Do you think that'll really matter to the side of your head?" says Jake through clenched teeth and with the nasally tone of a person with a recently broken nose.

"Jake, shut up," says Mulham. "Now, Sid, we don't have time to talk, not here. We need answers. Either way, I'll go home and will sleep soundly knowing America has been protected."

Sid leans over the chair, causing it to creak.

"America—or your own power?"

Mulham's jaw rises.

"First, tell me a few things," says Sid. "Are you proposing to just let me go back to my life, to my business?"

"Well, we can't have you continue all that. You've been digging too much into our informants' accounts. We'll bust the Chinese and Russian hacker rings and stop the corporate espionage when *we* decide it makes national security sense. We don't need you meddling in all those international affairs. You wouldn't believe how many problems you've caused over the years. That has to stop. Other firms clear stuff with us first. They play ball. But not you. No, you're special. So, after this, if we clear you, I guess you can go to work maintaining security systems or something. Maybe you can even be some company's IT guy. We don't care, just as long as you stay out of international affairs. We'll go over all that, and you'll have to sign things, but not here and not now. Right now we need a simple yes or no. Will you cooperate fully?"

"You mean, will I give you a blank check to run my life?"

"If you like, that is one way to put it."

Sid looks down at the .38 on the table and its cold blue steel and little plastic grips and snub-nosed barrel, and he gets angry. He knows Jake Halperin is there for the same reason the .38 was tossed on the table. They are both there to intimidate him. Halperin is a wild card who already made an attempt on Sid's life. Having him there adds authenticity to the threat.

But will they really do it? Yes, thinks Sid, they would. They would rationalize it as an act of patriotism. It's happened before. The only thing keeping him alive right now is they need access to all of his data. They need to know what he has done and who he has had contact with so they can mitigate the threat to their long-running program designed to pick and control presidents.

"It must be something to be able to look at and think about the inanimate object that will take your life," says Halperin.

"Jake, I told you to shut up," says Mulham with a low growl, but also with a little smirk, a tell that Halperin is acting the part of the bad cop he was ordered to play.

"Is this Neil Kuntz's plan?"

Mulham shakes his balding head. "We're not doing a movie confessional here before the big finale. This is real. Decide."

"But the decision has already been made."

"What are you talking about?" says Mulham, his eyes narrowing.

Sid sighs, straightens, looks into Mulham's snake eyes, and raises his voice.

"You are being recorded. Everything you've said is going live to multiple accounts."

"Bullshit. We've swept this place."

"Look in the elevator."

Mulham's dark eyes move to the elevator's partly open door. With a wave of his hand he motions the third agent, the muscle, to investigate.

The man opens the door the rest of the way, then pushes open the inner folding metal security door. He looks around and sees the phone off the hook. He picks it up and puts it to his ear.

"Let the record show an FBI agent is now holding the phone," says Sid in a loud, declarative tone.

The agent hangs up the phone.

"I didn't hear anything. No dial tone, nothing," says the agent.

"Pick it up and listen again," says Mulham.

The agent does so and then hangs it back up. "Now there's a dial tone."

"Who was on that line?" demands Mulham.

"A voice-messaging service. It was streaming to a number of cloud accounts," says Sid. "So, you see, my decision has been made. My team can bring out to the public everything that you've said." He pauses, holding Mulham's eyes. "It would be best if you leave now."

Special Agent in Charge Charles Mulham stands so fast his chair topples backward and bounces on the hardwood floor. His eyes go to the .38.

"We can still bury all this," says Halperin, desperation in his eyes. "That phone is fifteen feet away and in an elevator. How good can the audio be?" Sid knows the man is seeing his entire life, his hopes for a political career, everything, exploding to pieces in headlines and investigations.

"Maybe," says Mulham, frowning, "but we'll have to find out first. We'll have to take him somewhere until we can get the phone records in the morning to see who or what was on that line. Shit."

"Then what? You'll kill me somewhere else?"

"Damn it." Mulham pulls out a phone and walks into the kitchen.

After a moment of soft mumbling, Mulham almost shouts into the phone, "They can't *what*? You can't do that! You need to hold them. They'll come here.... I don't care you just got a call from Israel's U.S. ambassador or some general at Army Special Forces Command.... A Navy admiral?.... Who *are* these people?"

"Sounds like Gloria has been on the phone," says Sid, chuckling.

Halperin and the agent with the linebacker-sized shoulders are staring fire at Sid. He sees their thoughts clearly cascading into a lower circle of hell. They can't escape if there is audio out there of them threatening to kill "the cyber hunter." They could lose everything—their careers, futures, maybe even their freedom—all for this over-paid computer geek.

Mulham walks back into the dining room with the phone in his hand and the expression of a man standing before a jury on his strained face.

The door opens and closes downstairs. Footsteps are coming up the steps. Sid, still standing at the table, turns to see Neil Kuntz's sour face.

Kuntz is wearing a black trench coat over his gray pinstripe suit and has the jerky, stiff movement of a man about to do something desperate. He looks at Mulham and hooks a thumb toward the stairs. Mulham walks out of the room, down the stairs, and outside. The front door closes with a thud.

Kuntz takes Mulham's seat.

"Sit down, Sidney."

Sid just stands there, looking at the widow's peak, at the pouty lines on his late-middle-age face, at the puckering mouth, at the rat's nose.

"Sit down now, or this agent here will help you."

Sid glances at the big agent and smiles. He'd actually like to fight this man. It would be a challenge. Maybe a painful one, but he thinks he could take out a knee and then...well, he decides he'd rather talk to Kuntz than fight, as there are many things he'd like to know. He pulls out the chair and sits down.

Kuntz stares at Sid in an attempt at intimidation.

Sid doesn't speak to fill the void Kuntz purposely leaves in the conversation. He just looks back, waiting.

"Dammit," says Kuntz, "*Talk*. Tell me you're going to give us everything we want so we can clear this whole thing up without getting bloody."

"Bloody?"

"Don't play coy."

"Do you mean you're going to kill me?"

Kuntz's face twists up, then crumbles. He says, very slowly, "I'm out of patience. For national security reasons we need to know everything your team has found, and we need to know everything you've leaked and to whom you've leaked it."

"But I haven't leaked a thing.

"The only things I've put out there have gone into my columns, as well as the data I linked to in order to back up my claims," says Sid.

"Like hell. Your fingerprints are all over that dossier. We know you've released a lot of information. For the safety of our agents, because of U.S. national security interests I can't get into, you need to give us everything. You need to start cooperating. Sorting everything out will take weeks of interrogation and investigation of all of your accounts, but we need to begin right now."

"You have the wrong man."

"Shit, you could be convicted in any court of law with what we have," says Kuntz.

"So do it."

Kuntz looks away. When he speaks, his voice is low.

"You know I can't do that. The national security implications would be too great."

"Yes, I realize why you don't want your 'Vet the President' program to be known. I understand why you don't want the American people to know that your agency is a kingmaker, or the power behind the throne, or hell, pick your own metaphor."

Kuntz looks shocked. His stupefied expression shouts: *How does he know?*

A full moment passes as they sit there, eyes locked.

"We only do what must be done to save America," Kuntz says finally.

"Save? This is a democratic republic. The people elect representatives to make those decisions. Those elected officials are then, at least theoretically, controlled by the voters' will, as they want to remain in office."

"You naïve, idealistic little punk!" Kuntz shouts. "There is too much for the public to know. There is too much for senators or a president to understand and digest. They don't have the background to comprehend all the foreign and domestic threats. They can't fully understand all the data and the players and their motivations. It is too complicated for them. *We* protect America from foreign threats and from our elected representatives because *we* are the experts with the background and training. *We* do that. We have the information to do that. We are fast and responsive because we can work outside the political system. Democracy is slow, corrupt, and messy. Without us, it would crumble under the weight of the world."

"So, it's true, then. Like the Chinese government and so many others, you use information and your power to control who is elected and what officials can and can't do in office. You go after the thorns in your side, like me—and you even kill people when it suits your ends-justify-the-means approach."

Kuntz pounds a little fist on the table and snaps, "You damned fool! That's an overly simplistic interpretation, but I don't have the time or the inclination to debate the point. Give us what we want right now. I can have you over to the NSA in minutes to get the passcodes and whatever else they need. Do it now, and I'll even give you a window into what I know. I'll show you some of the recent national security threats, some of the attacks we've stopped, and more, so you can see how critical this power is, and how carefully we use it. But because of the audio you may have recorded here tonight, I need you to tell us where that is too. Because of you, there is no time to waste."

Sid spreads his palms. "That audio is out of my control."

"Like hell."

"You clearly don't understand how my system works."

"I know you're made of flesh and bone," says Kuntz before glancing at Halperin.

Halperin then nods to the big agent standing behind Sid. He comes up behind Sid's chair, grabs his left arm with his big left hand, and wraps his right arm around Sid's neck. Halperin moves behind Sid now and seizes his right hand. As Sid kicks and tries to squirm free, Halperin yanks his arms back and handcuffs him.

As the cuffs snap closed, Sid manages to pop up off the chair. The headlock around his neck tightens. Both agents and Sid fall to the floor in a squirming heap of arms and legs. The big agent now has a full Nelson on him and is tightening the hold. Sid is flopping like a hooked tarpon on a boat deck as he tries to turn toward his attacker, but he soon begins to black out as the headlock cuts the flow of blood off from his brain.

"Be careful, don't bruise his arms or face. We don't want any signs of a struggle," he hears Kuntz say, ice in his voice. "Now pick him up and put him back in the chair."

He feels the big agent get to his knees, bringing his almost-limp body up with him. Halperin and the other agent put him in the chair. The big agent releases the headlock, but stays behind him and wraps his arms around him with a bear hug. Sid comes around quickly, still woozy.

Halperin picks up the .38. Sid notices a smile growing under his bandaged nose as his eyes dart from the revolver to Sid.

"This won't hurt a bit," Halperin says with his nasally voice.

Kuntz leans in close and says, "Are you going to give us everything, right now?"

Sid is mostly awake now. He tries futilely to squirm free with his hands cuffed behind him and the big agent's arms around him and the chair, then stops struggling and attempts to calm himself, to control his breathing. After three deep breaths, he manages to say, almost placidly, "I will admit, that is an intriguing idea just now."

Kuntz's eyes narrow.

"But, once again," says Sid, "I'll have to tell you the die has already been cast, and there is nothing I can do about it."

"Okay, Jake. I'll hold his legs. Sidney, if you change your mind before your brains are blown out, all you have to do is nod and we'll give you a chance."

Kuntz kneels and tries to grab Sid's now kicking legs. Sid's knee smashes into Kuntz's nose, and he falls back on his butt. He tries again and is kicked again. He gets up a third time and shouts, "Dammit, hold him!"

Now the chair has slid out from under the table. Its legs are thumping as Sid rocks it back and forth. He stops momentarily and tries to headbutt the big agent by throwing his head back, but the man is ready and ducks to the side to avoid the blow.

Kuntz gives up and says, "Okay, Brent, put that headlock back on him. Just don't choke him out. I want him to have the chance to talk."

The big agent moves his right arm up to Sid's neck. Sid drops his chin in a vain attempt to block the move. The big agent's arms tighten; his left arm cinches down on Sid's neck.

"Okay," grunts Kuntz, using his shoulder and arms to hold down Sid's thighs. "Last chance."

Halperin steps forward with the gun, puts his left hand on Sid's left shoulder, and brings the gun up to Sid's head. Sid is trying to contort his body against the strength of the agent holding his neck. Desperate thoughts are telling him he has to stall. He needs time. He tries to nod.

"Get the angle right," screams Kuntz as he sees Halperin moving the gun back and forth.

Sid again tries to nod and speak. He doesn't know what he'll give them to stall them, but he knows he'll have to give them something.

"I think he wants to say something," says the big agent as he loosens his grip on Sid's neck.

Before Sid can say anything, there is shouting down by the front door.

Kuntz releases Sid's thighs, struggles to his feet, and stumbles backward. He shouts, "What now?"

Sid hears the front door open, then Paul Loring saying, "Agent Stephanie Baker is here, and she is insisting that she be allowed in."

"Shit, this isn't her case anymore," says Kuntz between deep breaths. "She is off the team."

He hears footsteps trotting up the stairs, then Loring's voice nearby. "She says you'll want to hear what she has to say. I think she is right." His tone is adamant.

"All right, dammit."

Loring goes back downstairs. The big agent lets go of Sid's neck. He steps back from Sid and stretches his arms as he breathes deeply. Halperin turns away and places the revolver in a drawer in a hutch.

Sid straightens in the chair, breathing hard and rubbing his neck. He hears the front door open and Loring say, "Okay." Then more steps on the stairs.

Special Agent Baker appears at the top of the stairs with a smartphone held up in front of her. She stops there and stares, her gaze drifting from Kuntz's bloody nose, Jake's wild eyes, the big agent, then Sid. Her gaze returns to Kuntz, who meets it with a deadly glare.

"Why are you recording this?" he demands, looking at her phone.

"I'm not," says Baker. "This is a livestream on Facebook. It is going viral."

"Impossible!" Kuntz stumbles back a step and looks desperately around the room, as if there is a person here he hasn't noticed, a person with a TV camera.

She walks right past Sid's chair without even looking at him and hands Kuntz the smartphone. He looks down at the screen, and his eyes widen. He is seeing himself on the screen, from a camera somewhere outside. He turns toward the glass doors in the back and looks out into the woods beyond the townhome's brick patio.

"I imagine my secondary team is back in those trees," says Sid. "They're probably wearing ghillie suits, as that's what Navy SEALS do."

"SEALS?"

"Well, retired SEALS, to be precise," says Sid, still breathing deeply, his face wet with sweat. "They run a private-security agency that does contracts for various companies. My team brought them in as soon as we got to town. Let me tell you, I sure hoped they were out there. Come on out, guys."

Shadows stand in the woods. They look like creatures from the Black Lagoon. Lights from the apartment complex below silhouette them and the cloth hanging off of every part of their suits, like leaves and vines, which sway gently as they stand. The monstrous shapes then walk forward, out of the woods and onto the patio, as the video on the smartphone closes in and the FBI agent standing out there steps aside, with a hand on a gun and the expression of a man going to the gallows. A motion sensor turns a light on the patio, and suddenly three men in ghillie suits with green paint on their faces can be clearly seen. They have cameras in their hands and are looking in through the glass doors. One is waving. They are all smiling.

Jorge walks out of the dark and stops beside them. He is not wearing a ghillie suit. He just got to the scene after being held by the FBI. He is also smiling and waving.

"*Nooo!*" screams Jake Halperin.

In a blur of a practiced motion, he pulls his SIG P320 out of his shoulder holster and points it at Sid and—

BANG-BANG!

The gunshots are deafening inside the dining room. Halperin falls back, and his gun hits the Oriental rug on the floor. He is screaming and holding his shoulder, and Special Agent Baker moves over him with her pistol pointed and her voice ordering him to lie on his stomach. She cuffs his hands behind his back. He is crying deliriously, "My shoulder, my shoulder...." She feels around his ankles and takes his backup gun and tosses them both onto the dining room table.

She then walks to Kuntz and takes her phone from his trembling fingers. With a swipe she takes the livestream of the room off the screen and dials a number with her thumb. "Yes, we need an ambulance. Gunshot wound. Not life threatening, but I think his shoulder is broken. Also, send the police. We have FBI agents on the scene, but need assistance."

Sid is still in his chair. Halperin had him cold. He should be dead.

He looks at Stephanie Baker and, for the first time, he doesn't give her his characteristic disarming smile. Instead, he has a wide thankful grin as he nods in appreciation. He then looks at Kuntz, who is shriveling up, pulling back into himself, pulling his arms in to hug himself in a sort of standing fetal position. His rigid hands then move up to his face to hide a gush of tears.

Sid turns away. He can't watch this.

Brent, the big agent, can't either. He has this dumbfounded expression of a man caught red-handed who didn't realize he was doing anything wrong. He stumbles back and sits on one of the brown leather couches. He is looking at Halperin bleeding on the floor and at Kuntz, who is now openly sobbing, and he doesn't know how to digest any of it.

"So you just watched as they were trying to point that .38 at my head?" says Sid to John and his team of former SEALS.

John smiles, which lifts the red beard all smeared in green paint on his big face. He says in a booming baritone, "It was such good TV that it was hard to stop watching. But really, it was all so sloppy, so unprofessional, that I had a hard time taking it too seriously, and I thought you'd start to talk just to stall them."

Sid shakes his head. "Jake Halperin already tried to kill me once today."

John laughs. "Yeah, I wasn't thinking about that."

"Did you get audio?"

"Yes. It isn't movie quality," says John. "Vibration-reading devices still have a lot to be desired—lots of background noise from distant traffic. But it'll work in a courtroom."

Jorge says, "You were doing a pretty good dance there, boss."

"I was going to have to give them something. Even if it was a fake something," says Sid. "In another moment, just to buy time. If I had to, I'd have even done my best to play the breaking man—tears, quavering voice, and all."

"Shit, I'd like to have that on video," says Jorge. "I've never seen you like that, Sid. Damn, what a missed opportunity."

"What a team I have."

They stop talking to watch Jake Halperin being wheeled out of the room on a stretcher and carried downstairs with a police escort. He face is flushed. He is ranting, but his mutterings are unintelligible.

John, Jorge, and Sid can't bring themselves to joke about seeing this FBI special agent break like this. They just watch solemnly as he is carried out.

"He is under arrest," says Special Agent Baker to the officers. "Make sure to record anything he says, as it can and will be used against him in a court of law."

A dozen police officers are in the townhome and outside now. Kuntz has been led away, and a team is photographing and searching the place.

As the SEALS stand around him in their green face paint and ghillie suits, Jorge says to Sid, "We have a lot. I mean a lot."

Jorge has an earpiece in, and he listens to audio via his phone. "Your bike kept recording, as did your helmet. It didn't stop recording until someone found the phone you tossed alongside the bike and terminated the Bluetooth connection."

"That worked?"

"It recorded what Neil Kuntz told Agents Halperin and Loring in that dead-end street. He told them they needed to get you back here to make you talk, and then to make damn sure you commit suicide. It's all here in his words."

Agent Baker steps between Jorge and Sid and overhears just enough to understand. She says, "Before you release anything more, can we talk?"

Sid nods.

"Thank you, Sid. I need you to come with me."

Just as she says this, Gloria enters the room, glowing with the radiance of the moment, as if a spotlight is following her. She overhears these last words from Agent Baker and says, "Hold on now, is my client under arrest? Are you kidding me? You people have done enough. *Enough.*"

"This is something else," says Baker, holding her hands up with her palms facing Gloria. "Will you come with me?"

Sid says, "Come on, Gloria. Let's go with Special Agent Baker. In fact, let's all go. Jorge, grab Adam. I think this will be good."

"Sure, he is outside getting everything on camera," says Jorge. "He is talking about doing a documentary."

It's a short drive. They leave the cul-de-sac and the townhome, still flashing red-and-blue from police lights. They are following Special Agent Baker's Maserati in the Bentley. Jorge is driving, Gloria is next to him, and Adam and Sid are in the back.

"Thank you, all of you; from the bottom of my heart, thank you," says Sid. Jorge nods and Gloria smiles warmly at Sid. Adam thumps Sid's left shoulder with a fist, but none of them say a word.

Bach's Cello Suite No. 1 is playing, and no one wants to speak in this melancholy moment as they relax in the leather seats. They drive down dark, quiet streets lined with three-story townhomes for a few minutes, go up a hill, and follow the black Maserati into the driveway of a stately home behind a walled-in garden off Arlington Ridge Road.

They park in a tiny circular driveway and step out into the darkness. It's well past midnight. The stars can just be seen through the city's light pollution. A motion sensor turns on a porch light, and they go quietly to the front door.

Agent Baker doesn't knock. She just opens the front door and stands aside to let Sid and his team walk in. A gas fireplace is burning in a den on the right, and two men and a young woman are seated on blue and white lounge chairs in the large room. Cigar smoke is in the air, and empty glasses are on mahogany end tables.

Senator Richard Haskins stands.

"Welcome, gentlemen and ladies."

They walk into the warm room and look around at the upscale living room filled with art, a chiming grandfather clock, comfortable furniture, and an older man with a trimmed white beard and lively blue eyes who is seated near the fire. Gloria recognizes him.

"Why, hello, Judge," says Gloria.

The judge puts his right hand on his right knee and his left on the arm of his chair and pushes himself up with a wince.

"Please, sit down," says the judge. "Who would like a drink?"

"Yes, I think we all could use one," says Sid as he walks to a liquor cabinet behind a small bar. The cabinet's doors are open. He begins dropping ice into glasses and asking for drink orders.

His eyes go briefly to the young woman in the room. "Lovely to see you, Carole."

"Hi, Sid."

"You are some actress."

"Men are an easy audience."

Sid smiles, shakes his head, then nods agreement as he looks down at the drinks he is making.

With bourbon poured over ice, and two martinis shaken and poured, and everyone seated on small couches and lounge chairs with drinks in their hands, Sid says to the judge, "Please, give us the story. I almost died to hear this ending."

"Oh, it's not an end, but another beginning," Senator Haskins says loudly as he laughs.

The judge says as he looks at Sid, "Good to see you're so easily at home. Especially given your ordeal tonight. Carole somehow—I don't pretend to understand technology—got your, what is it called, a 'live stream?'—to appear on that TV there. So, we watched it real time. Sound was a bit crackly, but we could make it out. Anyway, best TV I've seen in years. And what a plot twist. I never in all my years expected Kuntz to try that. We had to send Stephanie right over."

"I wish I were acting," says Sid.

"Oh, you did a marvelous job. By the way, as your attorney knows, I am Judge Harry Morgan, of the D.C. Circuit. As you may know, I also serve on the FISA Court."

The judge looks at Sid and then at Jorge, Adam, and finally to Gloria. "We'd like to raise our glasses in a toast to all of you."

Sid, Jorge, Adam, and Gloria look at each other uncertainly from their chairs, but follow along and raise their glasses and drink together.

"You all performed—as well as that team of former SEALS we didn't know about—better than we ever hoped."

"Hoped?" says Jorge.

"Right," says the judge. "We got together some months ago, after Special Agent Baker here came to Senator Haskins as a whistleblower. We talked it out. There was no way we could let Stephanie take the bullet for this. It wouldn't have even been a worthy sacrifice, as the system would have just eaten her alive. The FBI would have just leaked a little to cover itself—if even that were necessary, given the state of today's journalism—and then everything would have gone on as before. Aside, of course, from the destruction of Agent Baker's career and maybe life."

Senator Haskins says, "We couldn't let that happen."

"Quiet, Senator," says the judge. "You politicians are too long-winded, and it's already almost two in the morning. So we knew we needed another way. We met here in my den weekly as we thought and researched and discussed options. As I'd been duped into approving warrants for a lot of this, I felt I had to do something, even if it cost me my career. Then Special Agent Baker came to us with a pretty savvy suggestion. She proposed linking this thing to someone who'd make a damn big, self-righteous fuss about it; a do-gooder type who is both in the media and the tech world; a guy so idealistic and gung-ho he'd expose this thing or die trying. She proposed implicating you and your team here, Sid."

"Well, thanks a lot," says Sid, looking at Special Agent Stephanie Baker.

"My pleasure," she says, raising her martini again to Sid.

"So, another team member in our little cabal we'll not name put your fingerprints on that dossier and sent you that encrypted email."

"I can guess who," says Sid. "Tattoos on his arms. Hair just over his ears. T-shirts from Geeks.com. White Nikes. An NSA chap. I met him briefly. Kuntz and Jacobs brought him in to spook me."

"Well," says the judge, "forget about him, please."

Sid nods and the judge says, "To tell you the truth, I didn't think the ploy would work. I thought you'd think it was a prank or maybe that you'd just wait to see what happens. But, she was right, you threw your team on it and came down here with guns blazing."

"We tried to stop him," says Adam.

"We certainly did," says Gloria.

"We're glad he was too stubborn to listen," says the judge. "Though we did think we'd have to step in a few times, but you always managed to slither out of whatever they tried. We did help a little with getting you released from the FBI, and we got the rest of you released tonight as Kuntz tried to break Sid. That cost Special Agent Baker her spot on the team investigating you, though, and made them suspicious. And we were ready, albeit almost too slow, to stop them from making you commit suicide. But really, you were exceptional. Using the First Amendment, via all those cameras, at every turn has been sensational. But we do have to talk a bit about that."

"I never work for governments—it's a hard rule I've kept from the first day I started in this business—but you had me working both for and against the U.S. government without my knowledge," Sid says. "I wouldn't have thought anyone could play me like that."

"As I said, men are easy," Carole says.

"Very," Stephanie adds.

Sid holds up his bourbon to them nods, smiles, and takes sip.

"Now we don't want you to now rip down the entire system," the judge says. "We need to reform it, to cleanse it, to shine sunlight on it, not to blow it up. So we do hope you'll work with us on what to release and when to release it as we begin a Senate investigation and as the legal process unfolds on these rogue FBI and DOJ officials."

The judge pauses and makes eye contact with each of the team members until his eyes find Sid's.

After a moment of silence, Gloria says, "We'll need to talk a lot about that before we can give any answers, Judge Morgan. But, other than Sid, we've all served. We understand the mature sacrifice necessary. We just want to make certain we are not used to protect bad actors, or policies that can simply be turned back on to reinstitute this program once the spotlight has been turned off."

"That's exactly what we want," says Senator Haskins. "We need long-term reform and accountability. In the meantime, we need you to stay out there as a wild card for a while to keep the pressure up, as the establishment, and so many of their friends in the media, try to hide this. This fight is hardly over."

"Okay," says Sid in a big voice that controls the room. "I am open to that, but that conversation will need to begin with us being vindicated. I won't have my company, my people, and my reputation destroyed because of the actions of the Neil Kuntzs and Jake

Halperins of the system. We are not scapegoats nor martyrs. But yes, we don't have to needlessly burn down the system. I get that we don't want to hobble the intelligence agencies. They do a lot of important work, and, anyway, what might grow next in their place could well be worse."

"Well said," says Senator Haskins. "And I will be making a statement about you and your team this morning. I will ask you to testify before an open committee hearing, and I will tell the nation that you are patriots who did America an incredible favor. You were instrumental in taking out what is and has been an ongoing intelligence state coup. I'll have to choose my words more carefully than that, but you won't be disappointed with my tone. Of course, others will attack you."

"What'll be your story?"

"We decided," says the senator, glancing at the judge before looking back at Sid, "for now, we'll just say you were erroneously included in an opposition-research document the FBI was actively trying to suppress, in order to protect a sitting president, a president they prefer. We'll call it a cover-up and collusion between the FBI and the current president that goes back to when he was a candidate, so they could get him elected. That's a big enough scandal, and it's completely and provably true. We'll also cast doubt on the dossier's other sordid details. We'll call them biased and unsubstantiated as we focus on the political protection the FBI and DOJ gave this president. That'll create a political firestorm that will get partisan fast, and that's a tragedy of our system, but it'll keep the fire small enough for us to manage. A real conflagration just might burn the system down. That would please the Russians, but wouldn't do us any good."

"Right," says Judge Morgan, "and you and your team will be cast as the latest victims caught in the teeth of this cover-up, a cover-up so complete that they felt it necessary to kill you to keep their thumb on the political scales secret."

"Yes," says Senator Haskins, "that's actually an honest narrative—albeit with some necessary omissions."

"Omission is a form of lying, Senator," says Sid.

"True," replies Senator Haskins, "but you're not omitting the truth with this story, just the big picture. Is a photograph of a person dishonest because it also doesn't show what's to the person's left and right?"

Judge Morgan is laughing. "Attorneys, they try omitting facts to shape a favorable narrative for their clients all the time in the courtroom and in politics. But, in this case, I would accept this testimony in the courtroom, but would likely rule out the rest as unsubstantiated and irrelevant to the crimes at hand. We know you have a deep distaste for political expediency, Sid—it's part of why we chose you for this—but this isn't dishonest, just sharpened to the crimes at hand."

"And it'll still make you and your team the heroes of the tale," says Senator Haskins.

"Which is what you were," adds Judge Morgan.

"Okay," says Sid. He puts down the bourbon and feels the alcohol working its way into his weary body. "Let's talk about the details tomorrow. It has been a long week."

As the meeting breaks up, Carole walks across the room, sits on a coffee table in front of Sid, and puts her hands on his knees as she leans in close to say, "I am moving back to Iowa."

"Oh, that's wonderful," says Sid. But as he says this, he is surprised to feel a touch of disappointment in himself that is so deep it even makes its way into his voice.

"I am going to run the senator's reelection campaign. But I won't be coming back to this swamp," she says with a roll of her eyes toward Washington, D.C.

"You are very wise."

"Maybe," she says with a lovely smile and moisture in her eyes. "It's time, anyway. I'm going to find some tall, strong, straight-thinking man back in Iowa. I'll snare him and get him to the altar before he knows what fell on him."

"And he'll love every minute of it," says Sid.

She leans close and kisses Sid, then let's go of his knees and stands. He watches her walk back across the room as the agony of the realization that he is not man enough for her writhes inside of him. He realizes he really wishes he was.

Sid's eyes move past the senator's and the judge's, who are both watching him curiously, and meet Stephanie Baker's now catty scowl. Yes, there is definitely a hint of jealousy in her bright eyes. He smiles at her when he realizes this. He notices Gloria, who is standing next to her, shaking her head. She knows what he is about to do.

Sid approaches the FBI agent and says, "Are you going to work with me to make sure we use this information to reform, not destroy, the FBI?"

"Can you think of someone better?"

"Not even in the wildest depths of my imagination," says Sid.

Then he notices Carole across the room, smiling and shaking her head too.

"I can think of a better place than here, though."

"I'll bet," says Gloria.

CHAPTER

15

Sid's fingerhold on the white conglomerate rock is good. He swings, grabs a crack with his left hand, and lets his right toe push into a crease below. He is comfortable now, standing on his toe fifty feet over boulders in the spring sun.

He looks up into the nooks of the overhang. The Shawangunk isn't big. Its cliffs, though, meander for miles. He can get away up here on the quiet cliffs above his cabin and forget. He can climb up a boulder shoot, rappel down, pick a technical route back up—then have lunch looking east to the Hudson Valley, green now, or west to the Catskills, which are just far enough off that they look blue in the hazy distance.

He hears a beep in his ear and touches the phone on his belt to answer. A voice that makes him smile comes into his left ear.

"Mack keeps calling," says Stephanie with a happy, relaxed tone. "I finally picked up your house phone and spoke with him—weird to speak to him first person after hearing his voice via phone taps. Anyway, he says your column on your almost-'suicide' is going viral, and he wants you to promote it by doing some of the cable news shows that are calling."

"The hell I will."

She laughs and asks, "Where are you?"

"Up above, on the cliffs."

"Can I come up?"

"Tomorrow, we'll do a route together. I'm glad you slept in. Now, take a dip in the pool."

"Oh, but the water is chilly."

"Yes it is. Dive in and swim deep, then come up, step out near the waterfall, and slide into the hot tub. It's a sensation that'll lure in your appetite, and you need to be hungry for what I have for you tonight."

"Oh, lovely," says Stephanie.

He finishes the route up an overhang, swinging between holds, and then is on top. He sits down there and pulls his knees into his chest and feels the afternoon sun on his bare back. He chews on a piece of venison jerky pulled from a small pouch in his belt. He can just see the Hudson River, a bright ribbon in the afternoon sun. Emerald trees hide the towns and the roads between the mountain and the far-off river. The May sun is washing everything golden. Somewhere below a red-tail hawk makes its distinctive cry. The rising thermals bring the sound up to him, and he looks down to where his cabin is.

Yes, he thinks, up here things make sense. Everything from up on these hard, white cliffs is distant and simple. He knows he behaved as a fool, and, as fools so often do, he walked away a little dirtier, bruised a bit, with some abrasions on his career—but nevertheless intact, and with a growing reputation that has already attracted new business.

He begins to wonder what he might tackle next, but then stops. He doesn't care to think about it, not here, not now. Better to rest in the quiet times between. Better to let the breeze touch his skin and the sun to brown him as his mind rests and he heads back down to her.

THE END

About the Author

As a journalist, Frank Miniter has done everything from interviewing the president of the United States in the Oval Office to going in search of a mythical fish far up the Xingu River. He is a *New York Times* bestselling author and a writer known for hunting out the politically incorrect truth.